The Cruellest Month

The Cruellest Month

Hazel Holt

St. Martin's Press
New York

Library of Congress Cataloging-in-Publication Data
Holt, Hazel.
    The cruellest month : a Shelia Malory mystery / Hazel Holt.
      p.   cm.
    "A Thomas Dunne book."
    ISBN 0-312-05840-3
    I. Title.
  PR6058.0473C7   1988
823'.914—dc20   90-29336
                                                          CIP

First published in Great Britain by Macmillan London Limited.

First U.S. Edition: May 1991
10 9 8 7 6 5 4 3 2 1

For Tom and Kim

I would like to express my grateful thanks to Mr W. H. Clennell, the Assistant Secretary of the Bodleian Library, for his most generous advice and encouragement. And, indeed, to all the members of the Bodleian staff whose kindness and efficiency make that great library such an agreeable place to work in. I hardly need to add that the events and characters in this book are all (with the exception of the former librarian on page 157) entirely fictitious.

The Cruellest Month

Chapter One

I put the holdall with the unreliable handle down carefully on the pavement and reached inside the boot of the car for a cardboard box full of assorted groceries and thrust it into Michael's reluctant hands.

'Oh great,' he said, 'now I can open my very own supermarket.'

'Don't be such an ungrateful little beast,' I replied. 'You know you say the food in college is disgusting and that you're always hungry. And I *know* you've nowhere to cook anything,' I added as he opened his mouth to protest. 'I've just put in tins of corned beef and boxes of those little plastic cheeses that you like – nourishing protein.'

'What's this?'

'Vitamin C,' I said defensively. 'You're to take one every morning. The last thing you want this term, when you're taking your Finals, is one of your colds.'

'Oh, Ma, don't *fuss!*'

'A widow with an only child is allowed to fuss,' I said firmly. 'Now are you sure you don't want me to help you unpack all this lot and put it away?'

'No thanks. I shall leave it strewn around my room until it all beds down like compost. Anyway, I'm supposed to be seeing Hardwick in about ten minutes.'

Hardwick was a young man I had met in Michael's room several terms before. He had been sitting slumped in an armchair with his feet, in a disgraceful pair of trainers, propped up on the table among the (unwashed) coffee cups, drinking lager from a can. I had assumed he was a fellow student until Michael introduced him to me as his tutor. Oxford certainly has changed since my day.

'All right then, love. I'll drop in tomorrow after I've been into the Bodleian. If you're not there I'll leave a note about Sunday. I think Betty would like you to come over.'

'OK. Of course I'll come. I'd like to see Tony anyway. Cheers.'

He gave me a hug and, gathering up his possessions, disappeared through the small gate into the college.

Since I had, for the rest of the hour, that unbelievable rarity a free parking space in Oxford, I felt I should make the most of it and decided to pop into the Bodleian shop to replenish my stock of postcards (as I get older I find that I conduct more and more of my correspondence on postcards) and then have a little wander around Blackwell's – make myself at home again, as it were.

Outside the Sheldonian a young man in a blazer and a straw boater was sitting on a camp stool with a notice beside him which read 'Brideshead Tour of Oxford £2.50'. As I approached he raised his boater and said, 'Can I interest you in a tour of Oxford?'

I looked at him coldly and replied, 'That will not be necessary, thank you, since I am myself a member of this university.'

He grinned. 'Suit yourself,' he said.

I smiled back feeling rather foolish and hurried on. I suppose all graduates feel that they are somehow marked out and special when they are in Oxford and that this should be immediately apparent to all. To be mistaken for a tourist is definitely diminishing.

If I am honest, I must admit that my time at Oxford was the most purely happy of my whole life. That is not to say that I haven't had a marvellous life since – a happy marriage, a son, a sort of minor but satisfactory literary career – but there *is* something about the days of one's youth, when the world still had the dew upon it and anything seemed possible. I used to come to Oxford by train then. It was not long after the war and although petrol rationing had finished, it was still in short supply and often difficult to come by. In any case, my father was dead and my mother, like so many women of her generation, had never learned to drive. But I enjoyed the train journey from Taviscombe, the small West Country town where I lived – the little train to Taunton and then on to Reading. After I had changed at Reading for the slow, local train, my trunk and my bicycle safely in the guard's van, I would put away my book and enjoy the familiar litany of stations, each one bringing me nearer to Oxford – Tilehurst, Pangbourne, Goring, Cholsey and Moulsford, Didcot, Appleford, Culham, Radley – peering out of the window at the river as it wound lovingly through the countryside, craning my neck to see the University barges and then, always with a sense of excitement, the spires silhouetted against the sky.

But it was not, in spite of a continuing passion for English literature, Matthew Arnold's spires or his 'warm, green-muffled Cumnor hills', or Hopkins' 'towery city', or Hardy's Jude, or even Max Beerbohm's Zuleika Dobson that had made me determined, from my earliest teens, to come to Oxford. It was, in fact, Lord Peter Wimsey, Dorothy Sayers' hero, with his wit, sensitivity and, above all, his habit of quotation, who epitomised for me all that was romantic and glamorous in the world outside Taviscombe. My husband used to say, only half joking, that I only married him because his name was Peter and he went to Balliol. So I went up to Oxford in the early 1950s with my head full of romantic nonsense (me, Sheila Prior, actually *living* in the world of *Gaudy Night*) and Fate was kind enough not to disillusion me. I had a wonderful time.

One of my best friends, when I was up, was Betty

11

Rochester and we had kept in touch over the years. She had married a doctor who practised just outside Oxford (how I envied her that!) and I was godmother to her eldest child, Tony. I always stayed with her when I had any research to do in Oxford. I have published several books of criticism – mostly on minor Victorian writers, though there aren't many of *those* left to work on now – and I do a little reviewing for literary magazines, mostly American and Canadian; no one else seems to have the money to keep them going beyond the second issue. I had been asked to write a paper – 'The Home Front Novel: English Women Writers in the Second World War'. It wasn't really my subject, though an enjoyable one, so I was proposing to combine transporting my son Michael and all his gear to college with a little peaceful research in the Bodleian.

Betty (now Stirling) lived on the outskirts of Woodstock and as I drove up the Woodstock Road I was in my usual daydream of happiness at being in Oxford at the beginning of the summer term when all the trees are coming into leaf and the pink and white and mauve blossom bursts out exuberantly all over North Oxford. I looked for the great copper beech, a favourite landmark, on the corner of Lathbury Road, and there it was, its new leaves a soft haze of mauvish bronze. As I drove round the Wolvercote roundabout I was singing quite loudly. The Stirlings lived in a large modern house, but suitably built of Cotswold stone so that it merged harmoniously into the landscape. The gardens were large and full of unusual and beautiful flowers and shrubs. Robert, Betty's husband, was a fanatical gardener – I suppose it was a good way of relaxing from the demands of his patients, though, actually, he was very much an old-fashioned GP and simply loved house calls and long cosy chats, where he picked up all sorts of gossip, which he joyfully and most unethically relayed all over the village. He was immensely popular and I must say I often wished he was my doctor.

Betty read English at Oxford, as I did, and taught for a while. She and Robert were married when he was still at medical school and she carried on teaching for several years, even when Tony was born, to support them both until he was established. When their second child, Harriet, arrived she gave up her job and devoted herself to being a conventionally perfect doctor's wife – sitting on committees and raising money for medical good causes. A few years ago all this suddenly changed. When she was seventeen, Harriet ran away from home to join the Greenham Common peace women. Betty was horrified at first, but when Harriet came back – she always had a weak chest and a tendency to asthma and really wasn't up to living under canvas – Betty began to take up some of Harriet's ideas. Now she was deeply involved in Women's Rights as well as CND, Friends of the Earth, stopping nuclear waste and other related causes. Robert seemed fairly impervious to all this. He had never greatly cared about his creature comforts and now appeared to subsist on the endless cups of tea offered to him on his rounds and seemed quite happy to take a bit of bread and cheese out to his greenhouse when Betty decided that her time was too valuable to spend cooking and doing housework.

It was poor Tony that I was sorry for. Surrounded by cheerful, extrovert people, he seemed to shrink back into himself, so that he appeared more vague and tentative than ever. He was a slight young man, with fair hair and sad brown eyes behind gold-framed glasses (everyone else in the family had perfect sight). I once said to Michael that Tony reminded me of a wounded spaniel. He snorted. 'A water spaniel, perhaps – he can be really wet! Still, poor old Tony. I'm sorry for him, living in that household and with a sister like that! Imagine wearing a CND badge on your wedding dress!'

'Well, it wasn't a *church* wedding,' I said, 'and it was more of a caftan.'

'And scattering marigolds all over the place like that – it was deeply embarrassing. I didn't know where to look.'

Michael, like a lot of his generation is profoundly conventional.

'I don't know why she *married* that young man, anyway,' I continued. 'I thought proper feminists didn't.'

'She was making a *commitment*,' Michael explained patiently. 'And, actually, she and whatshisname, Hank, are into Greenpeace now. I saw Tony the other day in the Turl and he told me they're in New Zealand, going on from there to some atoll where there's a nuclear testing ground. *Aren't* you lucky to have such a boring, unadventurous son. *You'd* be worried to death.'

'Yes, I certainly would. Betty doesn't seem to bother, though.'

'She's far too busy saving the world herself to worry about her family – hence poor old Tony. Promise me, Ma, that *you* won't go all earnest in your old age.'

'No fear of that,' I said. 'I'm afraid I'm far too frivolous and light-minded, not to mention selfish.'

I really did admire what Betty was doing, though I must confess that I didn't look forward so much to visiting her nowadays, having got set in my ways and used to a more ordered life. Still, I was usually out working in the Bodleian during the day and I made a point of having a good, substantial lunch. Furthermore, I kept a small store of biscuits and chocolate in my suitcase.

When I arrived Betty greeted me enthusiastically.

'Sheila, dear, how lovely to see you! I'm so glad you're going to be here this week – we need all the people we can get for that demonstration at Brize Norton.'

Fortunately I was used to Betty's habit of taking over people, so I merely murmured that it was lovely to be there and mentally vowed that the wildest of horses would not drag me anywhere near Brize Norton. Actually, Betty has given me up as a bad job long ago and doesn't really expect me to join in any of her projects, although she always mentions them hopefully when I arrive, but it is tacitly agreed between us that I'm not really activist material.

'Am I in my usual room?' I asked. 'I'll just take my case up and unpack a few things.'

'Yes, dear, of course. I'm afraid Cleopatra's in residence there as usual. Honestly, she's getting worse, the way she's taken over that room. You are about the only visitor we can put in there now.'

Cleopatra was Tony's cat, a Burmese whose imperious disposition made her difficult to live with. Fortunately Betty, like me, was a doting animal lover and Robert – although professing dislike of all pets – had been known to make a special trip to Oxford market to buy a particular kind of fish to which she was partial.

I went up to the pleasant back bedroom overlooking the garden. There was a huge *Magnolia soulangeana* in full bloom outside the window and a mass of double cherry, both pink and white, just beyond. The room itself was impeccable, with gleaming furniture, fluffy white towels and fresh flowers. Mrs Rogers, who 'did' for them, knew what was due to the Doctor's position, even if his wife didn't, and Betty didn't seem to feel that it demeaned Mrs Rogers to do the housework, so everyone was happy.

As I entered the room I was greeted by a harsh cry and I went over to speak to Cleopatra who was in her usual position on the broad windowsill above the radiator. She was sitting on a pink velvet cushion (placed there specially), paws tucked neatly underneath, but as I approached she got up and arched her back, stretching her long legs and raising her head for me to pay my usual tribute. I stroked the soft fur under her chin and she gave a muted wail, then sprang down and stood beside my suitcase expectantly. I opened it and produced the cat treats that I always brought, breaking them into pieces for her.

15

She crunched them noisily while I washed my hands and tidied my hair.

'Are you coming down?' I asked. But having finished her treat she jumped into my open suitcase and, curling up on the one blouse I had that creased if you simply *looked* at it, regarded me smugly.

'Oh, Cleo!' I said resignedly and went downstairs.

I found Betty surrounded by posters and leaflets, which she was stuffing vigorously into envelopes. The kettle was shrilling noisily in the kitchen so I said, 'I'll make the tea shall I?' I came back with a tray, cleared a corner of the table and poured us both a cup.

'There are some biscuits somewhere,' Betty said absently.

'Not for me, thanks. Now tell me – how is everyone?'

Betty embarked on a long saga about Harriet's environmental activities in New Zealand. 'Though, of course she won't be able to go on the trip to that atomic island now that she's pregnant.'

'No! Oh, Betty, how lovely – you'll be a grandmother! When's the baby due?'

'Early in September.'

'Goodness. Well, they'll have to give up darting about the world like this now.'

'Oh no – Harriet will just put the baby in one of those sling things and take it about with them. It'll be frightfully good for it being part of *life* like that. Think of African babies on their mother's backs!'

'Poor little things,' I said, 'they always look dreadfully uncomfortable to me!'

Betty laughed. 'Oh, Sheila, you really are out of touch with modern life – it's all those dreary Victorian novelists of yours.'

'I suppose Robert's working too hard as usual?'

'He seems to thrive on it. Dawn till dusk. The matron at Evenholme was quite disagreeable about him calling to see old Mrs Clark at quarter to seven the other morning.'

'And Tony – how is he?'

A shadow crossed her face.

'I'm a bit worried about him,' Betty said. 'He's been very upset – well, you know how he takes things to heart.'

I was immediately concerned. If Betty, who was absorbed in other things, had noticed that there was something wrong then it must be serious.

'Whatever's the matter?'

'Something rather awful happened at the library and he can't seem to get it out of his mind.'

Tony worked in the Bodleian. Not in the old, grand Duke Humfrey part, but the New Bodleian, housed in the rather undistinguished building put up between the wars on the corner of Park Street. He loved his work and being part of the Bodleian and all that that implied. I believe he was very good at his job, since he was conscientious, reliable and meticulous, and Room 45 was his own little kingdom. Only there did he really seem to come alive.

'What happened?'

'There was an accident and a woman died. It was worse, really, because it was someone we knew. Do you remember Gwen and Molly Richmond?'

'Molly sings madrigals with your group doesn't she?'

'That's right.'

'I remember. They live in that lovely cottage at Great Tew. We went to a coffee morning there once. I met Molly but I don't think Gwen was there.'

'It was Gwen who died.'

'How awful. What happened?'

'Gwen was a librarian – retired of course. She must have been over seventy because she was up – I think she was at St Hughes – before the war. She was at the Bodleian for a bit and then, after the war, she worked abroad. She came home to England a few years ago and lived with Molly at Great Tew. Anyway, she was

17

asked to go back to the Bodleian to do something to some catalogue or other. She was working in one of those little rooms where they store things, in Tony's part of the library and some shelving collapsed and she was killed.'

'What a dreadful thing!'

'The trouble is, it was Tony who found her.'

'Oh, poor boy!' I exclaimed. 'No wonder he's upset – it must have been a dreadful shock.'

'Yes . . .' Betty hesitated. 'But I feel that there's something more to it than that.'

'What do you mean?'

'I don't know – he won't talk about it. He's always been so reserved. I really believe he talks to Cleopatra more than he talks to us!'

I bit back the obvious remark about not being able to get a word in edgeways – neither Betty nor Robert ever seemed to draw breath. But Betty really did seem to be concerned.

'Perhaps he'll tell *you* about it, Sheila. He's always been so fond of you.'

'And I'm fond of him,' I said warmly. 'I'll see what I can do. If he's a bit tensed up about it all – and it's only natural that he should be – it might be easier for him to talk to someone outside the family.'

The telephone rang and Betty went to answer it and I took the tray of tea things out into the kitchen. While I was rinsing out the cups Betty came back.

'That was Robert,' she said. 'He's going to be late. He's got to take old Mr Fraser into the Radcliffe – an emergency – and he doesn't know what time he'll be back. So we'll have something on a tray, shall we, and then I can get on with the minutes of the Environmental Protection meeting we had last night. Do you know, this new extension of the M40 is going to do *dreadful* things to that area round Otmoor – there are some really rare species . . . '

'What about Tony?' I asked.

'Tony?'

'Something on a tray.'

'Oh, he won't mind,' said Betty cheerfully, 'he's used to it.'

Chapter Two

When Tony got in he greeted me with quiet pleasure but barely spoke as we ate our cold pork pie and tomatoes. Not that there would have been much opportunity for him to do so since Betty plunged straight away into a detailed description of the trouble she was having with one of her committees. I was amused to find that the striving for peace and goodwill to all men (and women) certainly didn't seem to apply among committee members. The knives were out, apparently, for some wretched woman who had contrived to offend certain *other* members and a conspiracy was being hatched to get rid of her in some Machiavellian way that I couldn't actually follow.

'Come to think of it,' Betty said, 'I might just nip round now and see Margot Greenford. She's always in after six, and we can decide what to do next. You don't mind, do you, Sheila?'

She got up resolutely and gathered up some papers from the desk.

'I'll just go and make some coffee,' Tony said and slipped from the room.

When he came back, with Cleopatra winding herself round his ankles, his mother had gone. He put down a tray laid with the pretty white and gold coffee pot that Betty never bothered with, the matching china, proper coffee sugar and a lovely creamy gâteau. I exclaimed with pleasure.

'I got it from that shop in St Giles – I know you like them,' he said.

'Dear Tony,' I said warmly, 'that was very sweet of you. I absolutely adore their cakes. They are my *favourite* indulgence.'

We smiled at each other and Tony seemed to relax for the first time since he got in. He poured the coffee and cut the cake, giving each of us a large slice. Cleopatra, sitting beside me on the sofa, dabbed at my arm with a delicate paw and I broke off a piece of the creamy centre of the cake and offered it to her in my hand. She sniffed at it, looked incredulously at me and jumped down.

Tony laughed. 'Oh, Cleo,' he said, 'you are wicked!'

I laughed too – Cleopatra played the same trick on me every time and I always fell for it – and put the rejected piece of cake on the edge of my plate.

'Well,' I said, 'this is nice. It's been ages since I saw you. How's everything?'

'Pretty rotten, actually.'

'Your mother told me that there was a bad accident – a woman at the library and that you found her. It must have been beastly for you.'

He put down his plate as if he suddenly couldn't bear to go on eating.

'It was horrible . . . ' he said. His voice trailed away miserably and he sat hunched up in the chair, his hands locked together under his chin, a sure sign that he was upset. Although I knew that finding Gwen Richmond's body must have been upsetting for him (I don't suppose he had ever seen anyone dead before) I felt that alone was not responsible for his present distress. I was sure there was something else he couldn't bring himself to talk about.

'Look, tell me all about it – how it happened and everything. It often helps just to go through things that have upset us. I expect you've been squirrelling around in your mind, getting things out of proportion. We all do it.'

21

He gave me a wan smile, but a smile none the less.

'It was Gwen Richmond – she and her sister are friends of Mother's. Gwen used to work in Bodley years ago, and then she went abroad with the British Council – Italy and Greece mostly. When she retired she did occasional little jobs for us – updating catalogues she had worked on before, that kind of thing. When she – when she died she was working on the Anstruther Collection. They found a lot of new material in a private library somewhere in Northumberland, you may have read about it?'

His face suddenly became animated, as it always did when he was speaking about the library and his work there.

'Yes I did – they're more or less my period, some fascinating diaries and letters. I'd love to look at them some time.'

'Yes, you must. Gwen had almost finished cataloguing them and most of them have been dealt with by Conservation, so they'll be available soon . . . '

He stopped, took a deep breath and then continued.

'Anyway, Gwen was working on this collection. We're a bit pushed for space at any time and just at this moment we're having a lot of alterations done – new humidifiers, things to comply with new fire regulations – the lot! You can imagine, it's all a bit difficult. So Gwen had to work more or less where we could fit her in. She used to call herself an 'itinerant cataloguer'. She ended up working in Room 43 – it used to be one of the old stack rooms – all squashed up in a corner, surrounded by shelving. It houses a lot of old volumes, mostly local history, a collection someone left to the library that nobody really wanted, but he'd left some money as well, so of course . . . By rights we shouldn't have had them, but Carlisle wouldn't have them in his department so, as usual, they were dumped on us. As I said, it's one of the old rooms with wooden shelving and it simply wasn't up to the strain.'

He stopped speaking. Cleopatra, as she did every evening, jumped up and curled herself on his chest, breathing lovingly into his face. He smiled, stroked her head delicately with one finger and continued.

'Gwen seems to have wanted to get a book from one of the upper shelves. Nearly everywhere else the ladders are those metal ones that slide round on a rail – you know the sort of thing – but the ladder in Room 43 is a tall wooden one with a wide strip across the top, a bit top-heavy. Anyway, the ladder must have slipped and she caught hold of the shelving to steady herself and the whole thing came crashing down on top of her, books and all . . . '

'How terrible. And you found her?'

'Yes. It was a Friday afternoon and she hadn't been in the day before so I wanted to ask her if she was coming in on the Monday – she didn't come in every day. I opened the door, but it would only open half-way because of all the debris. I saw the shelving and the books and then I saw Gwen pinned underneath. I thought she was just badly hurt – her eyes were open, you see – but when I crouched down beside her I could tell . . . I think just the shelving wouldn't have killed her, but she was struck on the head by a great heavy book, calf-bound with brass edges. Horsley's *Britannia Romana* . . . '

This pedantic little detail moved me very much.

'Oh, Tony . . . '

'It was such a shock, you see.'

'Didn't anyone hear anything? Surely a crash like that would have made a fearful noise.'

'It must have done, but no one heard because Room 43 is right at the end of a corridor, through a couple of fire doors. I suppose someone might have heard a muffled thud, but we're used to a bit of crashing about because people aren't always as careful as they might be with the book trolleys.'

This was obviously a long-standing grievance and the

thought of it, I was pleased to see, did take away the stricken look he had as he remembered finding Gwen Richmond's body.

'Tony, dear, it was a really dreadful thing to have happened and you must have had an awful shock, but accidents do happen. You must try to put it out of your mind.'

He shifted Cleopatra's sleek fawn body to one side so that she could rest more comfortably and said uncertainly, 'I can't help feeling . . . '

'What?'

'Oh . . . well, responsible, in a way.'

'But it wasn't your fault. You couldn't know that it would collapse – *you* can't be expected to go around inspecting every inch of shelving to see that it's properly secure.'

'Yes, but— ' He broke off as his father came into the room.

Robert always makes me think of Richard III. I don't mean that he is a Wicked Uncle with a hunchback (though, in any case, I belong to the Josephine Tey/Guy Paget school of thought about Richard). No, I'm reminded of the line in the Shakespeare play when Richard talks about leaving the world free for him to *bustle* in. Robert definitely bustles. There is a small explosion of energy whenever he comes into a room.

'Sheila! How lovely! Is that coffee still hot? And do I see some cake?'

He embraced me warmly, poured himself some coffee and cut a wedge of Tony's cake all in one breath, as it were, and flopped rather dramatically into a chair.

'What a day! Well, I got poor old Fraser settled in the Churchill. It was a stroke of course. Wasn't it lucky I was paying him my weekly visit today?'

Robert always assumes you know exactly who he's talking about and I usually find it easier to let the whole thing flow over me, making little agreeing noises from time to time. Fortunately Robert never seems to require anything else.

'Well,' he continued through a mouthful of cake, 'I rang and rang and there was no reply, so I knew something must be wrong. None of the doors or windows was open, so I had to get in through that skylight thing in the conservatory,' he said triumphantly. 'He's got a splendid plumbago in there – I must see what I can do about it when he's out of hospital.'

Robert's collection of fine plants was largely built up by a sort of horticultural tithe that he exacted from those of his patients who were keen gardeners.

'Robert! Are you all right? It was really a very dangerous thing to do. You might have slipped and cut yourself very badly!'

'Nonsense. No problem at all. I just let myself down on to the staging and got into the house from there. He was lying on the bathroom floor – couldn't get up or anything. Still, he's all right now. His speech is coming back and we'll soon get some movement into that left side. I told him we'd have him back in his greenhouse in no time.'

I reflected that Mr Fraser might make a specially rapid recovery simply to get back to protect his plants from Robert's acquisitive hands.

'I rang that daughter of his. Now she'll have to come back and see to things. All that nonsense about a flat of her own in Oxford. It's only because of this man – he's married, of course. Naturally her father wouldn't approve . . . '

I used to worry about Robert's gossip, but I decided long ago that since I didn't know any of the people involved I could regard it as a continuing soap opera and enjoy it in the same spirit.

Robert put down his cup with a clatter and rose to his feet.

'Well, I'll be making tracks for bed. I want to read an

25

article on gallstones by that chap in Norwich – he's got some very way-out ideas, but he's very able – we trained together at Bart's you know. Does anyone want that last bit of cake?'

He scooped it up from the plate and went out of the room eating happily, scattering a trail of crumbs like the Babes in the Wood.

I laughed. 'Dear Robert, he doesn't change! Does he ever listen to a word anyone says?'

'Only to his patients, and they all seem devoted to him.'

'I'm not surprised – I should think that just seeing him would make them feel better – all that cheerfulness and vigour!'

'There are times when it might be a bit overpowering . . . ' Tony's voice died away and I felt that he wasn't just thinking of Robert's patients.

I stood up and collected the cups and plates.

'I want to wait up and have a chat with your mother when she comes in, so I'll see to these. You go on up. You look absolutely exhausted and I daresay you'll be up long before me tomorrow. Do you still go in at that ungodly hour?'

Tony was always at work long before anyone else and was one of the last to leave. As I said, it really was his whole life.

'Oh, the usual time – I like to be in early to get things done before we're really busy. How about you? When will you be in?'

I bent and picked up some of the cake crumbs from the carpet.

'I'll be in around mid-morning. Have you got anyone interesting in at the moment?'

I was always fascinated by the cross section of the academic world that foregathered in Room 45 and Tony had many stories of their eccentric personalities and behaviour.

'Not many people just now – mostly regulars –

a few members of the University, someone from St Andrews and a couple of quite nice Americans, though the American season hasn't really started yet – give it a couple of weeks and we'll be knee deep in them.'

'Oh, good. I like it best when it's quiet. I always get distracted by all the fascinating faces . . . '

'Can I get anything out for you to save time – have you got a list?'

'Bless you, but don't bother. I always use the time while I'm waiting for the books to arrive to catch up on my correspondence!'

'OK. By the way, how are the animals?'

'Fine. They're all staying with Rosemary. Electric blanket for Foss and consoling chocolates for the dogs – she is really sillier about animals than I am!'

We smiled at each other and Cleopatra, sensing that Tony was going upstairs, began her usual bedtime ritual. She leapt down and rushed up the stairs and down again, out into the kitchen and back into the sitting room where she went to ground under a chair.

'All right, Cleo.' Tony got down on his hands and knees and peered under the chair. A fawn paw emerged and batted at him while its owner uttered a low cry. Then a whiskered face emerged, pale golden eyes enormous with excitement. With one deft movement Tony scooped her up and swung her on to his shoulder. She lay there, completely relaxed, one paw dangling negligently down his back and with the sort of smug expression on her face that I have always imagined her namesake had as she drifted down the Nile in her golden barge.

Chapter Three

I have always loved working in libraries. Especially the Bodleian. When I was an undergraduate it always seemed positive proof that I was a scholar – look at *me*, I wanted to shout, here, in the *Bodleian* – and the atmosphere, especially in Duke Humfrey, of accumulated centuries of learning had seemed almost a tangible thing, the cloak of history thrown round my shoulders. Indeed, I do believe that it is the Bodleian rather than my own college, that will always mean Oxford to me. Now, in later years, that feeling had been reinforced – almost replaced – by a powerful sense of nostalgia. And not only nostalgia for my academic past. How many of today's (more earnest) undergraduates, I wonder, see this venerable building primarily as a place of assignation? Well, not quite assignation – more a place where you might, if you were lucky, catch a glimpse of the object of a passion (requited or not, as the case may be), and plan how to find yourself in the next seat, books cosily adjacent?

When you get your Bodleian reader's card you have to swear an oath, hearing your voice self-consciously reading out the words written on the card, agreeing to all the prohibitions required of you – you may not bring into the Library or kindle therein any fire or flame, or consume food or drink – but among all these prohibitions there is nothing to say that you may not, within the confines of this great library, fall in love. Which is just as well.

In my second year I had seen, usually sitting in the

same seat at the end of a row, a young man who had intrigued me. I was struck, first of all, by his extraordinary resemblance to Peter Wimsey. I got up from my seat, took a dictionary from the open shelves beside him, and, leaning on the radiator in its metal grille, studied him covertly. He was of medium height and slightly built, with a long face, straight fair hair and very beautiful hands – Miss Sayers' hero to the life! By an extraordinary coincidence (to one who knew *Gaudy Night* by heart) he was reading Sir Thomas Browne's *Religio Medici*. After that I haunted the library. One day I managed to get a seat next to him and was able to read over his shoulder the name and college on his notebooks: Rupert Drummond (immensely glamorous), Trinity (a disappointment – it should have been Balliol, but we cannot expect perfection in this life). He too was reading English, and also in his second year, so I saw him at lectures, shadowed him around Oxford and, through a young man I knew at Trinity, was finally able to make his acquaintance more formally.

It is a cliché, I suppose, that you never forget your first love, but it's true. Sometimes when I think of Rupert I find that I'm going around with an idiotic smile on my face, remembering that idyllic time in Oxford – simple pleasures, really, in those innocent days before the swinging sixties when holding hands in a punt and snatching a kiss in the shadows outside the college gates seemed infinitely romantic. It was, indeed, a perfect romance, perfectly (a cynic might say) rounded off by Rupert's tragic death in a climbing accident in the Alps the year after he went down, so that he remained in my memory as a young hero, a sort of Rupert Brooke figure, whose memory I still treasured like some rare piece of porcelain, fragile but enduring.

Rupert was very dashing and knew all the most interesting and fashionable people in Oxford and I followed happily along in his wake, marvelling that I, Sheila Prior, the daughter of a clergyman from an obscure seaside town, with no great beauty or wit to commend me, should be loved by such a god-like creature. One of the best things that Rupert did for me, and the thing that had the most profound effect on my Oxford days, was to introduce me to the Fitzgerald Circle.

Arthur Fitzgerald was a don at Trinity, whose influence and reputation as a scholar and critic ranked with those of C. S. Lewis and Lord David Cecil. He was known not only for his brilliant intellect but also for his wit and his eccentric manner. I had been to his lectures on Browning, of course, and had revelled in their mordant humour, such a delightful contrast to the bland treatment of English literature then prevalent in most girls' schools. He was reputed to loathe female undergraduates and his biting comments if any wretched girl crept into his lectures when he was in full flow were certainly terrifying. I had once wrung a grim smile of approval from him when I sat in the front row at one of his lectures on *The Ring and the Book* with an unwrapped birthday cake with 'Memento Mori' written on it in icing, but I had never expected to *meet* him.

He had gathered about him a band of – well, I suppose one might say apostles, whose social (he was a tremendous snob) as well as whose intellectual brilliance was impeccable. They met every Sunday lunchtime at his house in North Oxford to drink Madeira and wittily tear to pieces all the books, plays and pictures that had come to their notice during the previous week. Although I was thrilled I was absolutely terrified when Rupert took me along that first time, but Fitz (he despised the name Arthur and was always known by this abbreviation of his surname) was unexpectedly pleasant to me. He remembered my cake and praised my eccentricity, though I had brought it to his lecture only because I hadn't time to take it back to college, and it was unwrapped because in those days of austerity shops didn't wrap things up! Perhaps it was my

30

obvious vulnerability, like a puppy rolling defensively with its paws in the air, that brought out his carefully hidden kindness. Anyway, from that day onward he treated me with a grave courtesy, which I found very pleasing. After Rupert's death, when I was still drowned in grief, he replied to my brief heartbroken note with a beautiful and moving letter – I have it still – which helped me through that terrible time. A few years later he moved abroad – Harvard, I think, or it may have been Columbia – and we lost touch.

It had been spring when I first met Rupert and now, as I parked my car by Lady Margaret Hall and walked through the Parks towards the Bodleian, I had that idiotic smile on my face again. There were bluebells under the young trees and branches of blossom silhouetted against a blue sky. Even before ten o'clock there was warmth in the sun as I walked round the roped-off ground where, years ago, I had proudly watched Rupert playing cricket for the university. The benches round the pitch were empty, but one of the first matches of the season against a county side was due to start at eleven. I very much wished that I could stay and watch, but promised myself that I would leave the library early and try to catch half an hour of the match on my way home.

As I pushed my way round the revolving doors of the New Bodleian I was pleased to see that George was on duty behind the sort of counter, glass partition drawn back, checking readers' cards with his usual military precision, relieving people of their bags and handing out those cumbersome wooden tags in exchange. He has a fantastic memory for faces, though I am (I pride myself) an old friend, and of course he knows that Tony is my godson.

'Hello, George. How are you? No bronchitis, I hope?'

He gave me a broad smile and the ghost of a salute.

'Very nice to see you back again, Mrs Malory. Yes, I

31

did have a touch of the old trouble on my chest, but, you know my motto, best remedy for anything is hard work! And how long will we have the pleasure of seeing you in the library?'

'Oh, several weeks, I think. I've got quite a lot to do.'

'A new book is it, or an article?'

George had an encyclopaedic knowledge of his regulars' works.

'Oh, just an article. It will be lovely to be working in Room 45 again with Tony.'

'Yes, poor Mr Stirling. He had a very unpleasant experience – I expect he's told you about it.'

'Yes, indeed. What a terrible thing to happen. You must all have been very shocked.'

'It is not the sort of thing we are used to in the Library,' he replied severely. 'We had the police here and everything. Of course, no blame was attached, as they say, but it shouldn't have happened. The lady was getting on, you see. Should never have been allowed on a ladder at her age. But there's no telling some people.'

I got the impression that Gwen Richmond had offended him in some way and couldn't help probing a little.

'What was she like?'

'The sort of lady who was used to getting her own way, you might say,' he said with heavy restraint. 'Used to bossing foreigners about, I shouldn't wonder, when she was abroad.'

George, the old soldier, would not have taken kindly to what had obviously been an imperious manner. I wondered who else had found her unpleasant.

'She was always ordering Mr Stirling about, which was quite wrong, you know, Mrs Malory, since he is Staff and she was only Temporary . . . '

Here he had to break off since quite a little queue had built up behind me.

I handed over my shopping bag and said, 'I mustn't hold you up now, George.' I stuffed the wooden tag

32

into my handbag and crammed the catch shut with some difficulty. 'We'll have a proper chat later.'

I paused for a moment to juggle my handbag and folders into a more comfortable position, inhaled deeply that marvellous library smell that seems to be equally composed of dust, books and central heating and made my way along the corridor to Room 45.

It is a large room with high ceilings and tall windows all along one side and bookshelves along the other. There are reading desks, divided up into separate places with bookrests, in two long rows down the middle of the room, and card-index catalogues and desks for the library staff at either end. There is a general impression of lightness and pale wood and peace, and I find it womb-like and comforting.

There weren't many readers, so I was able to have my usual desk, near the door at Tony's end of the room, with my back to the windows. I put down my folders and looked about me. Tony wasn't there, so I found the catalogue number for the manuscripts I wanted to look at, filled in my green slip and took it up to the two girl assistants at the desk at the other end of the room. I knew one of them slightly – a short, jolly girl called Felicity who greeted me with a smile.

'Hello. It's Mrs Malory, isn't it. Tony will be back soon, he's just having his coffee break – he always goes early because he gets here at crack of dawn!'

She looked at my green slip and said reassuringly, 'These won't be long, they're in the stack room just down the corridor. Pamela will bring them to you.'

She gave the slip to the other girl whom I hadn't seen before. She was tall and very thin with straight brown hair cut in that rather depressing sort of fringe that barely clears the eyebrows. Unlike Felicity who was wearing a long cotton skirt and fringed top (what my friend Rosemary calls really *dreechy* clothes) she was dressed very conventionally. Indeed, her grey pleated skirt, white blouse and grey pullover, together with her generally youthful appearance, made her look like a schoolgirl. She seemed very nervous and shy and I wondered how Tony (also nervous and shy) coped with her.

I sat down at my desk and got out the Bodleian postcards I had bought the day before, spreading them out to decide which to send to an old colleague of my husband who was in hospital with a perforated ulcer. I was absorbed in my task and startled when I was addressed by the man sitting at the next desk.

'Pardon me.' The accent was American and the voice quiet, as befitted someone carrying on a conversation in a library. 'Pardon me for asking – but is it possible to buy those postcards actually here in the Bodleian Library?'

I turned and saw a tall, broad-shouldered man, probably in his middle sixties. He was almost bald but had a pleasant, rather square face, and his eyes were deep-set under heavy eyebrows and surrounded by laughter lines. I must say that, like many of my generation brought up on Hollywood movies, I am disposed to like Americans and fascinated by anything transatlantic, and I have several dear American friends, made in the course of my work. One of these, Linda Kubelik, once divided American scholars into the White Hats (those who, in spite of a long sojourn in the academic world, have retained their sense of humour and an ability to write readable English) and the Black Hats (who are all desperately earnest and only seem able to communicate in a sort of pseudo-sociological jargon). For no real reason I decided that this particular American was definitely a White Hat – practically, I thought, looking at his suntanned face, John Wayne himself.

'Yes – there's a Bodleian shop in the main building, through the quadrangle, by the statue of the Earl of Pembroke.'

Something – perhaps it was his rather attractive smile

– made me add, 'Actually, I'm going across there myself at lunchtime – I could show you where it is.'

Well, I told myself defensively, I *do* need another refill for my pen.

'That is very kind of you, I would be most grateful. What time had you in mind?'

'Oh, I usually go to lunch at about a quarter to one, is that OK?'

'That will be fine.'

The thin girl, Pamela, put the box of diaries I had ordered on my desk and I set to work. They were quite absorbing and I was absolutely immersed until I felt a light touch on my shoulder. It was Tony.

'Did you get everything you wanted?' he asked.

'Yes, thank you. Pamela – is it? – was very quick. I hardly had to wait at all.'

He smiled and moved away to his desk.

A little later I came up for air again and happened to glance down the room. Felicity had disappeared and Tony and Pamela were deep in a murmured conversation. Somehow I had the feeling that it was not about work but of a more personal nature. Pamela was seated at her desk, her head twisted round, looking up at Tony who was standing beside her. Something in her pose suggested a sort of desperation and Tony was bending over her protectively, almost as if he were shielding her from some danger. They were talking urgently together and I wondered very much what it was all about, but when the telephone rang and Tony picked it up and answered some query about photocopying quite normally I told myself that my imagination was running away with me as it so often does. Then I noticed Pamela get up and go quickly out of the room. After a few minutes I too got up and went into the ladies' cloakroom just down the corridor. She was there, leaning on a washbasin, and had obviously been crying. I pretended not to see her and went quickly into one of the cubicles. When I came out she had gone.

35

So I hadn't imagined things, I told my reflection.

I put on some more powder and lipstick and combed my hair, looking at myself critically in the cloudy mirror, and found myself glad that I was wearing a reasonably smart jacket and skirt and a new blouse in a shade of blue that does quite a bit for me. Then I shook myself mentally and went back to the problem of what was going on between Tony and Pamela. There seemed to be affection there – certainly on Tony's side – but the girl had looked more frightened of him than anything else, though I couldn't imagine how anyone could be frightened of Tony. Perhaps it was something about her work. Perhaps it had something to do with why he had seemed so upset the night before. My curiosity was now thoroughly aroused and I determined to find out what was going on.

Just before a quarter to one I gathered up the papers I was reading and put them neatly in their box, laid my folder and pencil on top and picked up my bag and gloves. My neighbour took a raincoat – I noticed with approval that it was an old but expensive Burberry – from the back of his chair and we went out together into the spring sunshine. Outside he stopped and said, 'I guess I should introduce myself. I'm Chester Howard. I used to teach at Harvard – still do the occasional class, though I retired last year.'

'Chester Howard?' The name was familiar. 'Oh, of *course*, you wrote that book on Edith Wharton – *Society and Sensibility* – really splendid!'

'That's kind of you to say so! Is it your period?'

'I more or less overlap. Though I'm not in your league – not an academic – strictly part-time. My name is Sheila Malory, by the way, though *you* won't have heard of *me*.'

'Actually, that is not so. I have read your book on Charlotte M. Yonge with great pleasure. I was delighted to learn so much about a writer too little known in the States, and was very interested in the comparisons you made with Ivy Compton-Burnett.'

36

He broke off suddenly and grabbed my arm just as I was about to step off the pavement. 'Watch out!'

A rogue cyclist, jumping the traffic lights, had swung round the corner from the Broad and nearly mown me down.

'Thank you,' I said, 'it gets worse every day. It's those cycle lanes – they all seem to think they're on some sort of racetrack.'

We negotiated the crossing with some circumspection and stood by the gates leading to the Sheldonian.

'I don't think Max Beerbohm would have cared greatly for those very restored Emperors,' Chester Howard remarked, gazing at them critically. 'They look like they were put there yesterday.'

'Yes,' I agreed, 'they've managed to make the stone look like plastic – very sad. Much nicer really to have them worn away and crumbling.'

We crunched our way across the gravel and walked through the arch into the Schools quadrangle. I always have a little glow of pleasure whenever I read the inscriptions over the various doorways: 'SCHOLA VETUS IURISPRUDENTIAE', 'MORALIS PHILOSOPHIAE', 'SCHOLA MUSICAE', 'SCHOLA VETUS MEDICINAE'.

We approached the main entrance to the Proscholium and went into the shop.

'There you are,' I said. 'Everything the heart could desire from postcards and wall-planners to Bodleian T-shirts. I always try to do some of my Christmas shopping here.'

'A veritable treasure trove,' he replied gravely. 'What are you doing for lunch? Would you care to join me?'

'That's very kind of you, but I'm just having a quick sandwich – I've got quite a lot of shopping to do. But thank you all the same.'

'Another day perhaps.'

'That would be lovely.'

'Well – see you back at the ranch!'

I smiled and went to buy the refill for my pen and he turned towards the racks of postcards.

As I made my way along the Turl I felt flustered and confused. There was no reason why I shouldn't have had lunch with Chester Howard, I had nothing else to do – the shopping was the usual convenient female excuse – but although I had instinctively liked him (perhaps *because* I had liked him) I had this urge to rush away.

'You are an idiot,' I told myself crossly, 'he only asked you to lunch, for heaven's sake!'

Now, because I didn't know where he was going for his lunch and I didn't want to be caught out in a lie, I felt obliged to make for the Cornmarket and do some shopping after all. As I surged uncomfortably round Boots, jostled by lunchtime crowds, I thought it served me right for being so irrational. I ended up having a hasty ham sandwich and cup of coffee at a café in the Market and went back to the Bodleian in a state of irritation.

Chester Howard did not return to his desk for quite a while, since his lunch had presumably been more leisurely and substantial than mine.

'Was your shopping successful?' he asked politely.

'Oh – yes – fine.'

I bent over my work again and was soon ready for the next box of documents. Usually Tony got things out for me, but I wanted a closer look at Pamela so I filled in my new green slip and approached her. She was wearing reading glasses so I couldn't see if her eyes were still red from crying but she certainly looked uneasy and upset. I gave her my bright reassuring smile – the one I use for confused, elderly ladies when I do Meals on Wheels – and it seemed to work, since she gave me a half-smile in return as she took one box of documents and handed me another.

As I turned to go back to my seat I saw that Tony was watching us both rather anxiously. I gave him a

38

bright smile too and he turned away in confusion as if he hadn't wanted me to know that he had been watching. I wondered if Betty knew about Pamela. Tony had had several girlfriends but I always had the feeling that they had been *found* for him, as it were, by Betty and Harriet. They were cheerful and rather bossy – what Michael calls 'save-the-whalers' – all obviously determined to 'make something' of him. I had watched with amusement Tony's quiet determination to remain 'unmade' and none of them had lasted for very long. Perhaps it was better, I thought with approval, that he should find someone that *he* could look after, someone even more tentative than himself – *that* might be the making of him! Pamela certainly filled the bill in that respect, but it didn't really seem to be a very jolly relationship.

About five o'clock I decided that I would indulge myself with half an hour's cricket in the Parks and packed up my things. I murmured a brief goodbye to Chester Howard, waved my hand cheerfully at Tony and retrieved my bag and shopping from George.

I crossed the street and went into Michael's college, which is directly opposite. He wasn't in his room and there was a piece of paper pinned to the door which read 'Out to Lunch' (a rather esoteric joke based on an American phrase that had caught his fancy), so I left a note in his pigeonhole reminding him to come to the Stirlings on Sunday and gave myself up to the pleasure of walking through Oxford on a sunny day in spring.

Chapter Four

I stood a little way off to enjoy the scene. It was the sort of picture that gets into tourist brochures: green grass, white figures moving in their timeless ritual, old trees with the fresh new growth of spring upon them and the pavilion, with its three gables and cupola splendid against the blue sky. Not many people were actually watching the cricket, just a scattering of enthusiasts around the edge of the field – there were a few undergraduates but most of the spectators were elderly. One of these elderly gentlemen seemed almost too good to be true – put there by some advertising man to add authentic English charm and eccentricity. He wore a cream alpaca jacket and a panama hat tipped forward over his eyes, his hands were resting on a walking stick and a dog was sleeping at his feet. One of the nice things about Oxford is the survival (taken for granted and unremarked upon) of such specimens of a bygone age. As I moved nearer to get a closer look at this particular one, I had the strangest feeling that I knew him and when I stood beside the bench where he was sitting I found myself calling out, in a much louder voice than I had intended, the name 'Fitz!'

He looked up, not startled, indeed with a glance of calm appraisal that seemed to imply that he was used to being hailed by strange females in just such a way. With a gesture that I remembered well, he raised his panama hat courteously.

'Madam?'

'Oh, Fitz, how lovely to see you, after all these *years*
– I didn't know you were back in Oxford!'

I sat down on the bench beside him and the dog, a King
Charles spaniel, raised its head from a contemplation of
its master's feet to look at me suspiciously.

'I don't suppose you remember me – it's been – oh
goodness – over thirty years! I'm Sheila Prior, Rupert
Drummond's friend.'

He replaced his hat carefully (I was pleased to see that
he still had his abundant hair, though its dark brown was
now heavily streaked with grey) and looked at me with
his head to one side.

'Sheila Prior?' He suddenly smiled and, raising his
hand in a dramatic gesture declaimed:

'What nymph should I admire or trust,
But Chloe beauteous, Chloe just?'

A middle-aged woman sitting on an adjacent bench
glanced at him sharply and the dog uttered a single
disapproving bark.

'My dear Chloe, how singularly pleasant to see you
again.'

Rupert and Fitz had always called me Chloe, after
the lady in Matthew Prior's poems. It felt very strange to
hear the name once more and a rush of memory and pain
brought quick tears into my eyes. To hide them I bent to
stroke the dog who nudged my hand approvingly with its
head.

'It's simply marvellous that you should be in Oxford
again. When did you get back? Where are you living?
What are you doing?'

'To answer your questions *de suite* or seriatim, if
you prefer: I returned (with the utmost thankfulness,
I may say) from the Americas last year; I am living
once more in Norham Gardens with Elaine (you may
recall my sister Elaine); as to what I am doing, I suppose

41

that splendidly vague word "research" would describe it in general terms.'

A short spatter of applause made us turn our heads towards the cricket as the University bowler finally managed (to his own surprise as much as the batsman's) to dislodge a member of the County side who had looked set to stay there for the next two days. Shaking his head with disbelief the batsman began his long walk back to the pavilion to brood about his averages and Fitz stood up.

'Let us take a turn about the Parks. Pippa here gets stiff if we sit for too long – and, to tell the truth, so do I.'

It seemed inevitable that Fitz should have named his dog from a poem by Browning.

'Does she really believe that all's right with the world?' I asked as we strolled across the grass towards a path.

'When she is with me, most certainly,' Fitz replied firmly. 'She was Elaine's dog – her name was Iseult, because, if you please, she had white paws – but when she attached herself to me – animals seem to do so – I felt obliged to give her a name that could be used in public without excessive embarrassment.'

He paused in apparent contemplation of a particularly fine may tree in full bloom.

'And what, my dear Chloe, are *you* doing in Oxford? I had heard – I cannot for the moment remember from whom – that you had returned to your seaside town and settled down to be a wife and mother.'

'I did, but Peter – that's my husband – died a couple of years ago and now my son is up at Oxford. I too am engaged in a little mild research in the Bodleian. At this *precise* moment I'm walking across the Parks to LMH, which is where I left my car this morning.'

'Then perhaps, since it is on your way, so to speak, you will allow me to give you a glass of Madeira and you can tell me about this *research*,' he emphasised the word ironically and I was once again a very junior member of

42

the Fitzgerald Circle, clutching an exquisite glass of old Bohemian crystal and trying unsuccessfully to defend an unfashionable and (to Fitz) unacceptable predilection for the works of Arthur Hugh Clough.

'That would be lovely.'

We left the Parks by the Norham Gardens gate and turned into the drive of one of the large Gothic houses near by.

'This must surely be the only house in North Oxford that hasn't been split up into flats,' I said.

'I am afraid that is so. Though even we,' he hesitated and lowered his voice as if about to impart some shameful secret, 'even we have been obliged to take in a *lodger*!' He turned and looked at me as if to assess the effect of this shocking revelation.

'Goodness!' I said feebly. I frequently found myself employing this useful but inane exclamation when I was with Fitz.

'When I was away in America it seemed unsuitable that Elaine should be virtually alone in the house – we had only one elderly servant – so Professor Mortimer – you may perhaps remember him – a mediaevalist – unsound on *The Knight of the Tour Landry* but perfectly adequate for the purpose we required, became our lodger. He died five years ago and since then our top floor has been occupied by Dr Marshall who is a physicist.' He made it sound like some exotic (and probably dangerous) animal. 'Fortunately we see very little of him. Like most of his kind he is very rarely at home. Apparently they have to – let me see, what is the phrase? – "book time on the laser" at the Clarendon Laboratory, frequently in the small hours of the morning. He also disappears for long periods to work on – can it be? – the electromagnet at Berne!'

Still talking he walked up the broad flight of steps, opened the heavy front door and led the way into another world.

I could hardly believe it, but nothing had changed since I last stood in that hall over thirty years ago. The walls were still panelled with dark wood, relieved by insets of De Morgan tiles, and a fine staircase of carved oak, with its red and blue Turkey carpet, led up to a landing whose stained-glass window featured Burne-Jones angels with lute and lyre.

Professor Edward Fitzgerald, named after the poet (a distant kinsman, Fitz would admit reluctantly) had also been a mediaevalist, but it was his wife who had been obsessed by the Arthurian legends – not from the pure Malory source, which might have been acceptable to her husband, but the Tennysonian version with all its romanticism and Pre-Raphaelite overtones. Not only had she insisted on calling her three children Elaine, Arthur and Lancelot, but she had furnished the house, a perfect specimen of Victorian Gothic, with wallpapers and fabrics from the workshops of William Morris and hideously uncomfortable wooden furniture, heavily decorated and sparsely upholstered from the same source. To my amazement, as we went into the drawing room I saw that here too nothing had changed. The wallpaper was faded as were the chair covers and curtains, which were also darkened with dust and age. The walls were still covered with a multitude of pictures, one of which I now realised was actually a genuine Millais and another an Arthur Hughes. The heavy painted dresser and corner cupboard stood where they had always stood, foursquare, defying time and change. The chairs, however, looked as uncomfortable as ever.

Fitz took some glasses and a bottle from the corner cupboard and I perched on the extreme edge of a sage-green *chaise-longue* with a wooden back on which was depicted a bemused Sir Galahad clutching a vessel of indeterminate shape, which I took to be the Holy Grail.

'This,' said Fitz, handing me one of the beautiful

Bohemian glasses which also seemed miraculously to have withstood the passage of time, 'is a rather delightful little Sercial, which I discovered in Sainsbury's.'

Such was the impact of Fitz's personality that for a moment I thought he was referring to the late, great George Saintsbury's cellar book and not the supermarket.

'Sainsbury's! Fitz – I can't imagine you in there!'

'But, my dear Chloe, the supermarket is the modern Eldorado – I discovered that in America – treasures of the Indies and, indeed, beyond – quite splendid! I do believe that shopping in supermarkets is the last great pleasure of old age. But, come, tell me what you are working on now. I greatly enjoyed your paper on Mrs Oliphant in old Robertson's *Festschrift* – a thoroughly scholarly piece of work and blessedly free of jargon.'

I glowed with pleasure, as I always did at any rare praise from Fitz, and told him about my work on wartime women writers. He made several helpful suggestions and I began to feel that I was back in time, discussing my essay with my tutor – except that my tutor had never provided a glass of Sercial, delightful or otherwise.

'But do tell me about your own research, Fitz. Is it still Browning?'

Fitz was considered to be one of the great Browning experts, but he hadn't published anything for a considerable time and it was expected that some monumental work on *The Ring and the Book* or some of the more difficult works was in the course of preparation, as they say.

'I have been taking a little *holiday* from Browning – something a little more *frivolous* – a study of Henry James in England. There, what do you think of that?'

'I am sure, Fitz, that you are the only person in England who would regard Henry James as light relief! But it sounds splendid – all the Lamb House period, I suppose?'

'Partly – though London as well. Actually, with regard to the Lamb House period, I am working quite closely with an American who is writing a book about E.F. Benson in Rye. There is a certain amount of overlapping – however, he is an old colleague from my Harvard days so we were able to reach an amicable agreement. He is working in the New Bodleian at present – you may have come across him in Room 45 – his name is Chester Howard.'

I explained to Fitz that we had exchanged a few words that very day.

'I refuse to make any trite comment about the smallness of the world,' he said. 'You will find him agreeable I am sure.'

'Aren't *you* working in the New Bodleian?' I asked. 'I'd have thought that the James material would be there.'

'Indeed it is, but I have been engaged for the last month on the tedious exercise of revising my 1963 edition of Browning's plays, writing a new Introduction and so forth, which meant that, sadly, I had to leave my new project and return to my old haunts – Duke Humfrey and the Upper Reading Room.'

'How sad – we won't be sitting side by side in Room 45. It is a pleasant place to work – blissfully warm. And, of course, my dear godson Tony Stirling is in charge there which is cosy. Do you remember Betty Rochester? She was up with me and read English too.'

'No face springs to mind.'

'Well, she married a doctor and lives in Woodstock (I always stay with her when I'm in Oxford) and her son Tony is my godson and works in Room 45.'

'As you say – cosy,' he replied gravely.

Something made me add, 'Poor Tony – he had a terrible experience the other day. You may have heard about it. A woman who works in the library died – some shelving fell on top of her – Tony found her.'

Fitz put his glass down on a black enamelled papier-mâché table decorated with stylised roses. It wobbled slightly as though the legs were uneven and he put out his hand to steady it.

'Oh yes,' he said, 'the accident in the Bodleian. I certainly heard about that. How distressing for your poor godson to make such a disagreeable discovery – *not* what one expects to find in one of the Great Libraries.'

'To make it worse it was someone he knew quite well, Gwen Richmond. Did you ever come across her? She was up at St Hughes just before the war.'

'Yes, I knew her. She was at one time a friend of Elaine. Can I offer you a little more Madeira?'

'No thank you, it was delicious, but I'm driving. Had you seen her lately?'

'Seen? Gwen Richmond? No, not for many years. It was not a continuing friendship.'

'No, of course not. She went abroad didn't she?'

'So I believe.'

There was a stiffness about his tone, more than his usual formality, which made me change the subject.

'How is Elaine?'

'She is in excellent health. Still, I regret to say, painting those appallingly whimsical faeries.'

Elaine was a talented artist who had made a name for herself as an illustrator of children's books, especially fairy stories – very elegant and stylised, a sort of English Kay Neilson. I had always loved her work and Michael's bookshelves, even now, held many of her books.

'Does she still have her studio in that enormous room upstairs?'

'As you see, nothing is changed. She is not here today, she had to go to London for some exhibition – artists lead such a *mouvementé* life don't you find? However, I am sure she would very much like to see you. Perhaps you would come to dinner – or luncheon if you would prefer?'

'That would be absolutely wonderful. But I must be

47

going. I'm sorry,' I suddenly remembered something, 'I ruined your afternoon's cricket!'

'It was a singularly dull match, but I find that sitting quietly there is an aid to digestion. Now you must give me your number and I will telephone you when I know what Elaine's plans are.'

When I got up to go he came with me to the door.

'Now, where exactly is your motor; would you like me to come with you to find it?'

'No, dear Fitz, it's only a little way up the road. It's been *wonderful* seeing you again, like old times. If only Rupert . . . '

'Ah, Rupert . . . ' He stood still, his hand upon the wrought-iron latch of the door.

'That was a long time ago. Do the years decrease the pain? I wonder.'

He opened the door and I went down the steps. At the bottom I turned to wave goodbye and regarded with affection the tall figure, leaning slightly on his stick. Really, like the house, he had hardly changed at all – a little stooped with age, though I felt that the walking stick (ebony with a silver knob) was an affectation rather than a necessity – and all those years in America had not changed the deep, drawling voice. Indeed, it was now almost a caricature of the old-fashioned academic. In a gesture that I remembered well, Fitz lifted his hand in a kind of benediction, which used, in the old days, to be accompanied by a murmured 'Bless you, my child', and went back into the house.

As I sat in the usual endless traffic jam that brings Oxford to its knees every afternoon from four-thirty onwards, I had time to think about my extraordinary day. The excitement of seeing Fitz again after so long – and how splendid that he knew Chester Howard, it seemed a most happy coincidence. And Gwen Richmond being a friend of Elaine. Thoughts of Gwen Richmond turned my mind to Tony and Pamela and the mystery (it hardly seemed too strong a word for it) of their relationship. As I edged slowly up the Woodstock Road towards the Pear Tree roundabout I wondered if I might be able to talk to him about it this evening. I was sure that he had something on his mind, something more than the shock of finding Gwen's body. It must be to do with the library since Pamela seemed to be part of it. I worried away at the problem but could come to no conclusion. Then I was finally past the roundabout, and the traffic, like water let out of a sink, swirled away in front of me and I had to concentrate on my driving.

When I got in Betty was in the sitting room rather shamefacedly putting a dish of cat food on top of the piano.

'I *know*,' she said, 'but when Tony's out Cleo will only eat her food up here!'

'Oh.' I was disappointed. 'Is he out this evening?'

'Yes, it's just us. Robert's got a BMA meeting in Oxford and Tony's seeing some friends.'

I wondered if Tony's friends were, in fact, Pamela, but I somehow had the feeling that Betty knew nothing about her, so I didn't ask.

'I've made some chilli,' Betty said, 'and I thought we could have it on our knees because I've videoed an old Dirk Bogarde film for us.'

Betty and I shared a passion for old British films of the forties and fifties and as we sat watching the black and white images of half-forgotten actors on the screen I suddenly felt a great wave of affection for her. In spite of all her new and (to me) alien interests, she was still one of my oldest and dearest friends, someone I was comfortable with, who would pick up my allusions and references, and with whom I shared so many memories.

As if catching my mood Betty said, 'Do you remember how *gorgeous* we thought he was in *Esther Waters*?'

49

'Oh, that was a heavenly film!'

We ate our chilli, which was excellent (Betty is a very good cook when she can be bothered) and watched the film in an atmosphere of happy nostalgia.

I went to bed early, before Robert or Tony had returned, because it really had been quite a day, what with Fitz and Tony and Pamela. Just before I fell asleep, I found myself wondering if Chester Howard would be in the Bodleian tomorrow.

Chapter Five

The next day was wet and horrible, not a bit like spring. The rain came in gusts, blown in your face by a cold, vicious wind. I abandoned all hopes of keeping my umbrella up, put my head down and ploughed miserably across the Parks, simply to take a short cut. The sunshine and blue skies of yesterday seemed part of another existence. The wet rope round the cricket pitch sagged depressingly and rain bounced off the benches. The wicket was covered, but there would obviously be no play today.

As I left my damp belongings with George at the desk I asked idly, 'Were you on duty the day that Miss Richmond died?'

'Indeed I was, Mrs Malory, and a fine old carry-on it was, too. The police were very good, tried their best not to disturb things, but some of our readers were very upset because, of course, they closed the Library. One lady – all the way from California, she was, and only had that one day in Oxford to check something she said – she was *very* put out. And Dr Lassiter, too, she said she wanted to verify something for an exhibition the following day. And then poor Mr Stirling – white as a sheet – a terrible thing to happen to him. Such a pleasant young man, very conversable and absolutely devoted to Bodley – I can tell you, he felt it very deeply, such a thing happening in his section. He is so keen on safety – fire regulations and such – not everyone is so conscientious, I may say –

and so concerned for his staff. *They* were very distressed too – well you can imagine – very nice girls. Miss Turner, especially – she was so upset she didn't come in the next day, so you can tell. Oh yes, Miss Richmond caused a great deal of trouble one way and another.'

Miss Turner would be Pamela. I couldn't imagine the bouncy Felicity being that upset.

'How wretched for you all.'

'Of course, it could have been worse. Term hadn't begun so there weren't as many readers as there might have been . . . '

He broke off as an impatient woman behind me thrust a Harrods shopping bag crammed with books and a very wet umbrella on to the counter.

'I'd better get on,' I said and moved to hang up my wet coat on one of the pegs in the passage beyond.

Chester Howard wasn't in Room 45 and I was aware of a distinct feeling of disappointment. Tony and Felicity weren't there either so I went up to Pamela who was sorting through some papers.

'Hello. You must be Pamela. I'm Sheila Malory, Tony's godmother.'

She was wearing the same grey skirt but with a red polo-neck sweater. Whether it was the bright colour near her face I don't know, but she certainly looked much less pale and wan than she had done the day before, almost cheerful, in fact. She smiled shyly and said, 'Yes, I know, Tony's told me about you. He's got a meeting this morning.'

She had a pleasant voice and I decided that I liked her. She handed me the box of documents I was working on and I became so absorbed in them that thoughts of anything else went right out of my head.

It was still raining quite hard when I went out to lunch, so I decided that I'd just nip across the road to the Kings Arms. The usual lunchtime squash hadn't quite developed, so that I was able to find a seat at a minuscule table with two chairs jammed up against it in a corner. I carefully put down my glass of white wine and regarded the contents of my plate with some misgiving. It sounds silly, but 'having lunch out' (I have to put it in inverted commas) is still a treat to me, as it is, I am sure, to most women who usually cook for themselves, and yet I am almost invariably disappointed. Not just in pubs. Even in quite grand restaurants I somehow find that what I have chosen isn't *really* what I want and the food that other people have on their plates always looks more appealing than mine. Pub food, though, is particularly hazardous in this respect, especially where an attempt has been made to provide 'interesting' or 'wholefood' menus. I know enough now to avoid the soggy quiche with its leaden wholemeal pastry or the vegetable lasagne drenched in tomato purée – everything that Michael sums up scornfully as 'carrot-cake food'. But perhaps I had gone too far the other way today with an enormous sausage enshrouded in some brittle-looking batter pudding and weighted down with a mound of pale chips. 'Toad'n'chips?' the girl behind the counter had asked and, thinking that there might be no nice filling chilli this evening, I had agreed.

Experimentally I ate a chip and decided that I was quite hungry after all. A voice behind me said, 'Is this place taken?'

I turned round and saw Chester Howard.

'No, do sit down. If you can, that is.'

He edged himself into the chair with some difficulty.

'I think,' I said, 'that if you sit sort of sideways with your legs *not* under the table you might manage it.'

'Yes, you are right. These little tables are not meant for the likes of me.'

'Not for the likes of anyone, really, except an anorexic dwarf.'

He had sensibly chosen to eat a couple of sandwiches,

which looked much more appetising than my now congealing sausage. I dug my fork into the batter which shattered into a thousand pieces and shot off the table.

'Oh dear – I think I'd better abandon the hole and just eat the toad.'

'The *what*!'

I explained about toad in the hole.

'Your sausages are one of my real reasons for coming to England so often. And marmalade. And scones. Though not necessarily together.'

We chatted about food and the weather and I found him very easy and pleasant to talk to.

'I gather that you come over here quite often?'

'I try to come at least once a year – I've been lucky with Leverhulme fellowships and suchlike – and now that I'm sort of retired I plan to spend more time in travelling anyway.'

'What about your family?'

'Sadly, I don't have a family any more. Just an apartment in Boston and a rather eccentric cat, at present staying with friends – his rather than mine, actually.'

'I know what you mean. They can be very demanding.'

Having finished most of the sausage, I pushed the remaining chips to the side of my plate and laid down my knife and fork.

'I believe we have a common friend,' I said. 'Arthur Fitzgerald.'

'Fitz? You're a friend of Fitz? Why that's marvellous!'

'I've known him for years – ever since I was up at Oxford – but I didn't know that he was back in England until yesterday. To be honest I can't quite imagine him in America. Though they do say that Boston is very like England.'

He laughed.

'Sure. They do say that – you should have heard Fitz on the subject. "The only things that Boston and England have in common",' his voice took on an approximation of

Fitz's drawl, "'is the plainness of the women, the inedibility of the food and a curious preoccupation with *tea*.'"

'Oh dear. That does sound like Fitz.'

'They loved him, though, and the more he insulted them the better they liked it. However,' his voice became serious, 'he is most able. His work on Browning is really seminal.'

'Oh yes, I suppose it is. I gather your present fields overlap in places.'

'Oh, he's told you about my study on Benson. Yes, a little, but of course his will be the more important work.'

'He seemed to regard it as almost frivolous,' I replied laughing.

'As you said, *that* sounds like Fitz. Do you know Benson's work?'

'I love the Lucia books – you're very lucky to have such a good excuse to go to Rye. It really is an enchanting place.'

'I have visited it in the past, of course, and fell under its spell, but I am glad to say that I will need to spend quite a lot of time there this trip. Meanwhile I'm enjoying working in the Bodleian very much. It's a very civilised atmosphere, don't you find? And they are so efficient and helpful in Room 45.'

'The young man there – Tony Stirling – is my godson, so I'm prejudiced, of course, but, yes, you are right. I love the Bodleian – it reminds me of my youth.'

'How fortunate you are to want to be reminded – I try not to think of mine.'

He levered himself to his feet.

'I am going to have the other half of this strange flat English beer. Will you have another glass of wine?'

'My son would be appalled to hear you call it that – *that*, I must tell you, is Real Ale. And no, I don't think I'd better have any more wine else I'll fall asleep over my notes this afternoon. I'd love an orange juice though.'

He fought his way through a scrum of students and returned with two glasses.

'Tell me about your family,' he said. 'You say you have a son?'

'Yes, he's in his last year here.'

'Reading English?'

'No, History, like his father.'

'Your husband is an historian then?'

'No. He is – he was a solicitor. He died just over two years ago.'

'I'm sorry.'

'I'm over it now, I suppose – or as much as one ever does get over losing someone one cares for very much. And I've got Michael.'

'What is he going to do when he graduates?'

'He doesn't seem to know – it's a bit worrying. I think he might stay on and do research if his results are good enough. I gather his tutor is quite hopeful.'

I thought of Hardwick and his grubby trainers and sighed.

'The academic world is changing so quickly, I don't really know if that's what I want him to do.'

'Worse in the States. Tenure. All those dreadful books pouring from the more obscure university presses simply because you don't get tenure if you don't publish *something*! Perhaps Pope was right.'

'Pope?'

'Didn't he say to an aspiring poet: "Young man, if your father has a trade, follow it!"'

'Poor young man! But in Michael's case it mightn't be a bad idea. He'd make a good solicitor.'

'I'd like to meet him. Perhaps you'd both have a meal with me one evening.'

'We'd like that.'

'Where are you staying in Oxford?'

I explained about Betty.

'How fortunate you are. I am very fond of the country

round Woodstock, and it's very handy for you to have a godson in the Bodleian.'

'Yes indeed. Though poor Tony – I don't know if you heard – there was a dreadful accident there last month and one of the staff was killed. Were you in Oxford then?'

'Yes, I was, though I was not in the Bodleian at the time – I had gone up to London that day with a friend – but I heard about it when I went in the following week. Shelves collapsed, I gather, on some unfortunate woman.'

'Something of the sort, though I think it was more complicated than that.'

'Really?'

'Well, not complicated exactly, a large book fell on her head as well. Anyway, it was Tony who discovered her. It upset him very much . . . '

'A dreadful thing to have happened.'

'Yes. Not what one expects in the Bodleian. Poor George – do you know George? He sits in that little cubby-hole and takes your bags and checks your reader's card – he feels it very much. "What in our house!" – that sort of thing. Which reminds me,' I looked at my watch, 'I must get back.'

We eased our way through a group of young people who were engaged in a noisy argument about the relative merits of Bizet and Meyerbeer and emerged thankfully into the fresh air. It was still raining.

Chester Howard put up his umbrella and politely escorted me across the road to the door of the Bodleian.

'I have to go to Blackwell's to pick up some books I ordered. I'll see you around.'

Betty had warned me that she and Robert had to go to 'some dreary function' that evening and that Tony and I would have to fend for ourselves. I returned to find Betty in despair.

'This wretched dress! It must have shrunk or something – it's split at the shoulder. And my hair's fallen apart!'

'Hang on, give me a needle and cotton and stand still – I'll sew it on you. Fortunately it's on a seam so it won't show.'

I drew the edges of the black lace together as best I could and Betty suddenly giggled.

'Do you remember when you sewed me into that dress for the Commem. Ball at Corpus and I had to wake you up in the small hours to cut me out of it?'

'You always did eat too much and burst out of your clothes,' I said severely. 'Stand still, for goodness sake or I'll drive this needle straight into you. There. How's that?'

Betty craned her neck to look over her shoulder.

'That's marvellous. I must remember not to breathe.'

'Actually you'd better take a scarf or wrap to put over your shoulders in case you come apart again. Now, let's see what we can do with your hair – I'll get my electric curling tongs.'

By the time she was ready and Robert had rushed in, hurled himself into a dinner jacket and hustled Betty away I was feeling quite exhausted.

'Put on your coat,' I said to Tony when he came in. 'I feel in need of a large meal. I am taking you to Shipton-under-Wychwood to eat some of that delicious roast lamb they have at the pub there.'

Driving through the Wychwood Forest we talked of general things – where Tony was going for his holiday (Greece), how Michael might do in his exams (quite well if he kept his head), and what Harriet and Hank might call their baby (Little-Friend-of-all-the-Earth?). Only when we had finished our garlicky lamb did I introduce the subject I really wanted to talk to him about.

'Tony . . . I feel somehow that there's more to this Gwen Richmond business than you've told me. I don't

58

want to badger you, but I can see that you're worried and unhappy about it all and – well, it *might* help to tell someone. You know that anything you say will be safe with me. I'm so fond of you, my dear, I *hate* to see you so wretched.'

Tony stirred his coffee with immense care.

'Yes, you're right, of course. There is something. But – well – there's no one positive thing that's wrong, just several little things that don't seem to add up.'

'Such as?'

'To begin with, I can't understand why Gwen should have been on that ladder in the first place. I mean, there's nothing on those shelves that she would have wanted – it was all British antiquarian studies – not her subject at all.'

'I suppose something might have caught her eye and out of idle curiosity she went up the ladder to get it down?'

'Well, that's the other thing that puzzles me. She wasn't wearing her glasses.'

'What do you mean?'

'Her sight wasn't particularly good – I mean, she couldn't possibly have read the titles of books on the top shelves without her glasses and even when she was up the ladder she would have needed them to read the writing on the spine. She had sort of bifocals you see.'

'And she wasn't wearing them when you found her?'

'No – that was the first thing I saw – her eyes, open and staring – almost as if she was *accusing* me of something – if that doesn't sound too fanciful.' He picked up his wine glass, stared at it without drinking and then put it down again.

'But surely,' I said, 'her glasses would have come off when she fell.'

'That's what I thought had happened. But later I found them in their case on her desk, under a pile of books that had fallen off the shelves.'

'I do see – it does seem odd . . . '

'She was rather vain, you see. She hated to wear her glasses if anyone was there – she'd whip them off if she heard you coming into the room. She could just about manage without them, but if she'd been cataloguing for a couple of hours I'm sure she would have been wearing them.'

'So you think that someone was in the room when it happened? That someone pulled the shelves down on top of her – someone *murdered* her? Surely that wouldn't have been possible?'

'I think that was to make it look like an accident. I think she was hit on the head.'

'Well, yes, you said that that book – the something or other Britannia – fell on her?'

'But it *couldn't* have, because books of that size aren't kept high up, they're always on bottom shelves.'

'Oh dear,' I said inadequately. 'How awful.'

'Yes. You see how it is.'

'But what about the police?'

'They seemed to accept it as an accident – they weren't to know about the glasses and the book. They said the screws holding the shelves on to the walls must have come out when she clutched at them when the ladder fell. I don't know if they found them – it was pretty chaotic in there even before the shelves came down. And there was an inquest – it all seemed straightforward.'

'You didn't mention any of those things to the police?'

He looked at his cup.

'No.'

'Well,' I said briskly, 'I don't suppose you thought about it at the time – what with the shock and everything – and I dare say it was difficult to come out with it after everything was cleared up, as it were.'

'Yes.'

He hesitated.

'No – that's not it. If I'm honest, I must admit that

60

I didn't want anyone to look into it too closely. Partly because of what any sort of scandal might do to Bodley – I mean, tabloid newspapers – you can imagine the headlines: "The Body in the Library" – that sort of thing – and the way they drag things up . . . '

'What sort of things?'

He started to talk very quickly.

'Gwen wasn't a very nice person – she offended a lot of people. Her manner was – well, difficult – and she had an unpleasant habit of always knowing something to everyone's disadvantage, if you know what I mean.'

'I know just what you mean.'

'She'd been very strange for a little while before she died. Once she made some odd remarks about things coming home to roost . . . I don't know what she meant, it sounded very melodramatic . . . and the past catching up with people.'

'She sounds very unpleasant but do you know that anyone would have actually wanted her *dead*?'

'No – I don't know – not anyone one actually *knows* – no that wouldn't be possible.'

He spoke vehemently, almost as if he was trying to convince himself.

'Things like that don't happen to people like us?'

'Something like that.'

'They do, though.'

'Yes.'

We sat in silence until a sudden burst of laughter from a group of locals talking to the landlord at the bar broke the tension between us.

'Tell me about Pamela,' I said. 'She seems very nice. Am I right in thinking that she is a particular friend of yours?'

I chose my words carefully and was rewarded by a grateful smile.

'Yes she is – a particular friend. And very nice.'

'Does she live in Oxford?'

'She lives with her mother in a flat at Wolvercote. Mrs Turner, her mother, is an invalid – it's all a bit difficult for Pamela – well *you* know what it's like, you will understand.'

I, too, had had an invalid mother until three years ago.

'Poor girl, it can be a strain. Is she fond of her mother?'

'Oh yes. Mrs Turner is a marvellous woman – very brave and cheerful – Pamela is devoted to her.'

My mother had been brave and cheerful too. She had also been witty, compassionate and quite exceptionally life-enhancing. I hoped that Pamela was as lucky.

'I see her sometimes. I give Pamela a lift home and pop in to say a word. She gets pretty lonely by herself all day. I wonder . . . ' he hesitated. 'I wonder – would you come with me one evening?'

'Of course, I'd be delighted.'

I was very flattered that Tony trusted me with this part of his private life and I was certainly curious to see how he fitted into the Turner household.

Chapter Six

I was able to form my own opinion about the Turners the very next day. I was up early for breakfast having been woken by a dawn emergency telephone call for Robert, who I observed from my bedroom window striding down the path towards the garage, his black bag in one hand and what seemed to be a currant bun, from which he took enormous bites, in the other.

'Was Robert *really* eating a currant bun this morning?' I asked Betty as I put some bread in the toaster.

'It could have been,' she said yawning. 'He just snatches up what comes to hand when he has an early call – once it was a couple of cold roast potatoes.'

'How does he do it?' I marvelled. 'After a late night, too, he seemed to be fresh as a daisy! Toast for you?'

'More than I am. Nothing to eat for me. Just tea.'

'Was it a good do?'

'Not as bad as I expected and I was able to have a really useful chat with Leslie Robertson, who's organised this group over at Enstone – we're going to get together – both groups – over the by-pass protest.'

'Oh good – you're up,' Tony said to me as he came into the kitchen.

'I can give you a lift in and back again this evening if you like, Sheila. I'll be leaving in about half an hour.'

'Splendid! I'll just have this bit of toast. Oh, by the way, Betty, Cleo's in my bed so I'll have to leave it.'

'Dreadful animal!' Betty said absently. 'Don't worry, I'll see to it later on when she comes down.'

As we drove in Tony said, 'Would you like to come with me to the Turners' this evening? It seems a good opportunity.'

'Won't it be rather short notice?' I asked.

'We'll just put our heads round and say hello – nothing formal.'

As we walked to the car that evening, Pamela said shyly, 'Thank you for coming to see Mother. She gets very few visitors. We don't have many friends here – Mother moved to be with me when my father died last year. We used to live in Leamington.'

'Were you up at Oxford,' I asked.

'Yes, I was at St Hilda's – I read English – and then I was lucky enough to get this job in the Bodleian . . . ' She broke off, as if she was uncertain about something, then continued, 'Tony's told me about your mother and how you looked after her for all those years. Was it very difficult?'

'No, not really. I was lucky – my mother was a wonderful person and I loved her very much, so I never felt that I was making a sacrifice. And then, of course, Peter, my husband, loved her as much as I did. There was never any question of where she would make her home. We wanted her with us.'

'You were lucky to find someone who felt about things as you did,' Pamela said wistfully.

'Yes I was. Peter was very special.'

The Turners' flat was in a red-brick, barrack-like block just off the main road to Wolvercote. The rooms were small and box-like with low ceilings and metal window frames. I could imagine the condensation running down them in the winter. It was a ground-floor flat and I felt that it might well be noisy. Sure enough, as Pamela turned the key in the door, we could hear the whirr of a Hoover being used in the flat above.

64

'Mrs Organ-Morgan's at it again,' Tony said and they both laughed.

'The woman upstairs is obsessively house-proud,' Pamela explained. 'She always seems to be sweeping or Hoovering. It's a little joke we have about her.'

I smiled benevolently on them both.

Mrs Turner was sitting in an orthopaedic chair by the window – just as my mother used to do. But where Mother had had the trees and hills of Exmoor to refresh and delight her, Mrs Turner's view consisted of a row of garages and a line of parked cars. But the windowsill was crowded with flowering pot plants, the meagre little room was comfortable with old-fashioned furniture and the cream-emulsioned walls were almost covered with pictures – mostly old prints. Mrs Turner rose painfully to her feet and came and took my hand.

'How very kind of you to come, Mrs Malory. It's so nice to see a new face.'

'I'm so pleased to meet you.'

I led her back to her chair and she settled herself with a small sigh.

Pamela said, 'Will you have a glass of sherry or would you rather have tea or coffee?'

'I think I'd like a cup of coffee, please,' I said.

'Won't be long,' Tony said and followed Pamela out into the kitchen, leaving me alone with Mrs Turner. She was a small, thin woman, about my age. Her hair was still a rich dark brown but her face was lined and drawn, the result, I knew of years of pain. Her hands were twisted and strapped up with supports and she wore trousers, as my mother had done, to hide the strappings on her legs and ankles, as well as for the additional warmth. But her expression was cheerful and lively and we chatted happily about her plants and how she missed her garden.

'I couldn't do much, by the time I had to leave – this wretched arthritis makes things very difficult. But, then you know all about that. Tony told me about your mother.'

'It is a terrible thing and they still don't seem able to find a cure – though there are things, I know, that can help.'

'Hospital waiting lists are so long . . . still I manage to keep occupied.'

She reached down and produced a knitting bag from beside her chair.

'I can't do tapestry work any more but I can just about manage to do a bit of knitting. Fortunately my hands aren't as bad as my poor feet.'

She smoothed out the front of a pullover. It was knitted in a very complex stitch and beautifully done.

'What a complicated pattern!' I exclaimed. 'It must be very difficult.'

'Following the pattern's quite easy – my brain hasn't gone yet! – but it takes a long time to do a row. It's for Tony, you see. He's been so wonderfully kind to Pamela and to me. Do you know, he was worried about me using the electric stove when Pamela is out – I warm up something that she leaves me for lunch, bless her. So he managed to find this microwave oven – just like new. A friend of his mother's was getting rid of it, he said – she was going to have a bigger one. Well I wasn't sure if I could manage it at first – I didn't quite understand about the Standing Time.' She brought out the technical phrase with pride. 'But Tony is so good at explaining things, so patient. He's a wonderful boy!'

Her face lit up as she spoke and she gently stroked the knitting on her lap. I could imagine how painful it must be for her just to hold the needles and the thought of the affection that made her persevere made my throat prickle with tears, as it does when I see things that move and upset me, like old ladies whose supermarket baskets hold only a small tin of soup, a packet of biscuits and

66

six tins of cat food. I admired not only Tony's kindness but his tact as well.

The young people came back with the coffee and some of Pamela's shortbread and we were quite a jolly party. It was lovely to see Tony as the centre of that little household, to see how he grew in stature and authority as they deferred lovingly to him, and how gentle and affectionate he was not just with Pamela but her mother as well. He was happy here – all the sweetness and generosity of his nature had found an outlet at last, and I resolved to do everything I could to make this happiness last.

I was not surprised the next day when Pamela, handing me my document box, asked if I would have lunch with her.

'I have to go rather early, if you don't mind. About twelve?'

'That'll be fine – places are always much emptier then.'

I chose to go to a rather health-foody place called Salad Days, partly because it had a lot of quiet corners where we could talk undisturbed, and partly because Pamela didn't look like the sort of girl who would feel comfortable in a pub – certainly not a noisy Oxford pub.

We settled ourselves down with our bowls of salad, our rolls and our fruit juice (orange for Pamela, apple for me) and I said brightly, 'Well, this *is* nice!'

Eating salad these days is really hard work, especially since they've taken to putting in chunks of raw cabbage, apple and intractable pieces of red and yellow peppers, not to mention nuts and fibrous bits of fennel. We chewed away in comparative silence for a while and then Pamela seemed to brace herself and said, 'Tony's told me so much about you. I mean, I know that he's very fond of his parents and sister but . . . '

'They are rather *busy* all the time, yes, I know. Tony's always been very special to me and I do care very much about his happiness.'

'Has he told you that he's asked me to marry him?'

'My dear! How marvellous!'

'But I've said no.'

'But why? He's obviously devoted to you – and – well, it seems to me that *you* are very fond of *him*.'

'That's it – I love him too much to ask him to take on an invalid mother-in-law as well. And I could never leave my mother.'

I remembered using the same arguments to Peter and I remember his answer:

'My dear girl, you and your mother have built up this wonderful relationship – if you will let me be part of that, then *I* will be the lucky one. Anyway,' he gave me his lovely one-sided grin, 'you know I'm only marrying you because your mother won't have me.'

I told Pamela what he had said.

'That was a marvellous thing to say.'

'I'm sure Tony feels the same way. Besides if he really likes your mother and she likes him – and I'm pretty sure that's the way it is – then there's no reason why it shouldn't all be a marvellous success for all three of you. It seems to me that we only ever hear about the times these things *don't* work out – I'm sure that thousands of couples are as happy as Peter and I were in that situation.'

She smiled and said, 'Tony told me to talk to you about all this – I expect he knew how convincing you would be.'

'I'd be very happy to think I had convinced you.'

She was silent for a moment and then she said tentatively, 'There's something else . . . something quite serious.'

She took a sip of her orange juice as if to fortify herself to continue.

'I've done something wrong, something very foolish. I think I must tell you.'

'You can tell me anything you like – I won't repeat it to anyone.'

First Tony, now Pamela – I seemed to be a sort of confessional.

68

'You've seen Mother, how bad she is. Well, I heard about this new treatment – an artificial ankle joint – like an artificial hip – and her doctor said it would certainly benefit her, she would be able to get about, she might even be able to go out again. It seemed wonderful. But there's a two-year waiting list and we couldn't afford to have it done privately. We're pretty hard up, you see. My father had a bookshop in Leamington, but he wasn't a very good businessman. When he died – he had a heart attack – there were bills and things, and by the time we had sold the house there wasn't much left and no pension for my mother. We can just about get by on what I earn and Mother's invalidity allowance. I've got a little saved up, but nowhere near enough to pay for the operation. But, oh, I *did* want her to have it!'

'I know how you must feel. We were very lucky. *My* father died when I was still at school, but my mother had what was known in those days as "private means" so we never had any money worries. She always had the best treatment that was available. You must feel so frustrated to think that she *could* be helped . . . '

'That's just it! And that's why I did it.'

'Did what?'

'Stole some valuable books from the Bodleian.'

Automatically I noticed that she didn't say Bodley, as Tony did, and then I realised what she had told me. She gave a wry little smile at my astonishment.

'Yes, you're right – it was totally out of character – I couldn't believe myself what I was doing.'

'But I thought that all the books had those little stamp marks on them?'

'Only after they've been accessioned. When the books arrive they are held in one of the accession rooms to await processing. It's a chance for the staff to have a look and see what's come in. Anyway, I spotted these books – they were part of a collection that had been left to the Bodleian, but it was all a bit of a jumble, there wasn't a catalogue of any kind. I knew that they were rare – I remember my father telling me what similar ones had fetched at auction several years ago.'

She had been talking quickly, as if by telling me as rapidly as possible she could slur over what she had done, now she spoke more slowly.

'It was just before twelve o'clock and for once the room was empty – the person who was working there went to lunch at twelve and I managed to scoop them up and hide them among some other books I was transferring on a trolley. I had the most dreadful fright. Just as I'd got them on the trolley the alarm bell rang. I was sure they'd found out and would be looking for me. But then I remembered it was a Thursday and they test the alarm every Thursday. You can imagine how my heart was beating! I took them into a stack room that we don't use and smuggled them out through the back staff entrance when I went to lunch.'

She looked at me beseechingly.

'*Please* don't think too badly of me – I wanted *so* much to help her!'

'I don't think I could blame you. I would probably have done the same thing myself.'

'When I got them home I felt terrible. I knew I shouldn't have done it, that I couldn't go through with it – trying to sell them. I suddenly thought about what *she* would say – she'd know I couldn't have got the money honestly. I didn't know what to do. I didn't dare to take them back – I was afraid of being caught . . . So I told Tony.'

That must have been a great test of his love, I thought, since his loyalty to the Bodleian was the cornerstone of his life. 'What did he do?'

'He was wonderful. I could see how dreadfully upset he was, but he never said a word of blame. He got the books back himself so that they were never missed. But then something awful happened.'

70

'Something else?'

'Gwen Richmond – she saw me take the books, I don't know how – I suppose she must have been round the corner of the room and I hadn't seen her. I told her that I'd put the books back – I couldn't let her know about Tony, of course – and that I'd never do anything like it again. I *begged* her not to tell anyone. At first she said she wouldn't and that she hoped I'd learnt my lesson. But then, a few days later, she said that she really ought not to let it go and that it was her *duty* to tell Mr Frankau – he's the Keeper of Western Manuscripts. She was playing with me, like a cat with a mouse. I honestly didn't know where I stood. It was terrible! It went on like that for a couple of days and I was getting desperate. I told Tony that I would go and tell Mr Frankau myself – but I needed the job so badly and if he sacked me I wouldn't have any sort of reference – I mean, how could he . . . Anyway, I'd almost made up my mind, when she had that accident and died. It sounds really awful, but when I heard I said, "Thank God!" – wasn't that dreadful? But you can imagine the relief!'

So Tony hadn't told her of his suspicions about Gwen Richmond's death and she had no reason to suppose that it was anything other than an accident, miraculously releasing her from an agonising situation. Or had she? But no – stretch my imagination as I might – there was no way I could see Pamela murdering anyone.

'You must both have been very relieved,' I said inadequately. 'And it's over now. You must put it behind you. You'll never be tempted to do anything like that again, the books are back so there's no harm done. Your job is safe.'

'I'm giving up my job in the Bodleian.'

'But why?'

'Tony's found me a proof-reading job with the University Press – I can do part of it at home, which will be better for Mother.'

So Tony had settled his conscience. I knew that for Tony stealing a book from Bodley was an unforgivable crime – a betrayal of trust. Pamela – even his much-loved Pamela – couldn't stay on there after what she had done. She was sensitive enough to understand his attitude and to feel that there was now a cloud over their relationship. I set myself to dispel her doubts.

'You poor child! What a time you have been through!'

She obviously hadn't been expecting sympathy and her eyes suddenly filled with tears.

'I hadn't intended to tell anyone, ever, but I'm glad I did. And Tony will be glad too. I don't know if I should tell Mother.'

'No!' I said sharply. 'No, you mustn't tell her. Just thinking of what you would have done to help her . . . she would feel so dreadfully responsible. No,' I continued, 'you must put it all behind you – make a fresh start – you and Tony and your mother. Tony did the right thing – you'll feel much better when you're away from the library. You must marry him – for his sake as well as for your own.'

'You really believe that?'

'I do.'

'Then I'll do it. Oh, thank you! I'm so glad that I told you about it – I feel so much better . . . '

I could see that she *would* be able to put the whole thing behind her. She had shifted her burden to Tony and, to a lesser extent, to me with the confidence of a child who believes that the grown-ups can make everything all right. Tony would have to be strong and wise for all three of them, but this new Tony, I felt sure, would be perfectly able to cope.

I said as much to him – though not exactly in those words – that evening after supper. Betty was glued to the telephone rallying her troops for some planning enquiry and Robert was using a rare free evening to do some potting up in the greenhouse, so we had the sitting room to ourselves.

'I'm so pleased that she told you everything,' Tony said. 'It means that she feels safe with you.'

'I like her so much,' I said, 'she's exactly right for you. And I like her mother, too. I think I was able to explain how Peter and I felt about Mother living with us – I think she felt reassured.'

'Thank you, Sheila,' he said warmly. 'I knew that if anyone could persuade her you could.'

'So when can I buy my new hat for the wedding?'

'Quite soon, I think. There's no reason to wait and I'd like to be able to look after them properly. I've got quite a bit saved up for a deposit on a house – we'll need a garden for Cleo . . . ' He broke off and stroked her head. 'That's the only thing that worries me – how Cleo will take it. I mean, they both love cats, but Cleo is rather . . . well . . . you know.'

'I think you will find that Cleo will be thrilled to have a doting full-time slave in Mrs Turner who is around all day to pander to her every whim.'

He laughed. 'You're probably right.'

Cleo, sensing that we were talking about her, jumped off Tony's lap and began, quite deliberately, to sharpen her claws on one of the chairs.

When she had been reproved, I said, 'I can understand now why you didn't really want to stir up any sort of enquiry into Gwen Richmond's death. But it does seem likely that if she tried that sort of blackmail on Pamela she may well have tried it on someone else – and with quite different results!'

'You're right, of course. I was so concerned about Pamela I didn't really think it through. All that stuff about the past catching up with people . . . '

'What exactly did she say, and when? Can you remember?'

'It was one morning when I was having my coffee break. She sometimes used to come and sit by me. It sounds silly, but I think she rather liked me. She

73

had this sort of joking, flirtatious manner – it was a bit embarrassing.'

I could imagine that Tony would have found it so.

'I got the impression that she had just met someone she hadn't seen for a long time – years and years – and that she was planning some sort of revenge. I'm sorry to be so vague but it was veiled hints and general remarks, nothing concrete. She did say something about it never being too late to right a wrong. It sounded a bit melo-dramatic – but then she *was* a bit over the top, if you know what I mean. Very opinionated, very vehement. In a way she wasn't really talking to *me*. I got the impression she'd just seen this person, whoever it was, and she was so worked up she had to talk about it – however obliquely – to *someone*.'

'So you think it might have been someone she'd seen in the Bodleian – a reader, perhaps?'

'Well, yes, it could have been – I mean, it was almost as if she'd just seen whoever it was, that morning.'

'When was this? I mean, how soon before she died?'

'About a couple of weeks, I think. I could probably tell you exactly if I look up my desk diary – I can usually date things by remembering what I was working on.'

'So she might have been blackmailing someone she'd known in the past – someone who'd done something wrong – something criminal even. And she wouldn't want money, like an ordinary blackmailer, but power over another person.'

Pamela had said that Gwen Richmond had played with her like a cat with a mouse. That kind of thing, used against a really desperate person could lead, and perhaps had led, to tragedy.

'Yes, that was Gwen all right. If she couldn't dominate people by her personality – and it was a pretty strong one – then she'd try to find out something discreditable about them – quite little things, but niggly – and hold it over them. She never said anything outright, just hints or snide

74

comments. It didn't make for a very pleasant atmosphere, as you can imagine. We all tried to avoid her as much as possible. After all, she was only with us on a temporary basis – she would soon be gone.'

'And it seems most likely that someone helped her on her way! She does sound most unpleasant. I can't imagine that anyone would grieve for her. What about her sister, though? You know her, don't you?'

'Molly? I've met her a few times at madrigals and fêtes and things. She seemed very nice – not a bit like Gwen. I don't really know how she felt about Gwen's death. They'd only been living together for just over a year – since Gwen came back from Greece.'

'If Gwen *was* murdered, whoever did it took a tremendous risk. I mean, he snatches up a heavy book and hits her over the head and then takes the time to unscrew the shelves and bring them down on top of her with all the books crashing around . . . suppose someone had come in.'

'Room 43 is rather out of the way, so I don't think anyone would have heard the crash. And, as I said, we all tended to avoid her as much as possible – kept well away from her. *I* only went to see her because I needed to know if she was going to be there for a meeting on that particular Monday – it wasn't something I often did. And as for unscrewing the shelves – it wouldn't have been all that difficult. It wasn't a large section of shelving, and it was quite old. I had a look after . . . after they cleared everything away, and the shelves were only secured in a couple of places, it wouldn't be difficult to unscrew them.'

'I've only just realised – whoever did it must have been a member of staff or a reader. I mean, with George on the desk keeping his beady eye on things someone couldn't just have wandered in off the street.'

'And just at the moment, with all the alterations and upheavals going on, the only readers are in Room 45.'

'Can you check on who was in that day?'

'Yes, of course, and I'll see if I can find out where the rest of the staff were – though if it was someone Gwen had only just met again after a long time that would rule them out, because nobody new has come since Gwen came back.'

'I wish I'd known her – it's difficult to try and picture a person you've never met. I do feel I'd like to know more about her . . . '

I broke off as Betty came into the room looking very pleased with herself.

'There. *That's* done. I think we're going to have a very successful enquiry. I managed to round up quite a lot of waverers. By the way, Sheila, do you fancy taking a few hours off tomorrow and coming to a coffee morning with me at Great Tew?'

'Great Tew?'

'Yes, Molly Richmond asked me to go, and, since I've just talked her into coming to the enquiry, I thought I'd better say yes. Do come and swell the numbers.'

I looked at Tony and he smiled.

'Yes, Betty, I'd love to come with you tomorrow.'

Betty looked surprised but pleased. 'It's in aid of new equipment for the village school. It really is so important to keep the village schools going, they are the heart of the community. The headmistress is going to drop in and tell us about the curriculum and how the school fits into the local area plan. I'm sure you'll find it all very interesting and informative.'

I avoided Tony's eye as I said dutifully, 'Yes, Betty, I am sure I will.'

Chapter Seven

We drove past the signpost that says 'To The Tews', leading to Great and Little Tew. I love those signposts. You seem to get them mostly in Oxfordshire and Gloucestershire. As well as The Tews there are The Barringtons and The Rissingtons, though I think my favourite is The Pluds, who must surely be cartoon characters. The Tews, on the other hand, are rather suburban, I think. 'We're going to dine with the Tews and the Barringtons and the Rissingtons are coming in after for bridge.'

We drove into the village, past the school, which seemed very flourishing to judge from the number of children engaged in some sort of PT exercise on the green outside, and turned left down the hill.

There were already several cars outside the cottage and we had to park quite a distance away. As we walked back towards the cottage I asked Betty if Molly Richmond had been very upset about her sister's death.

'It's hard to tell. She's such a placid person, you don't feel anything has much effect on her. I went to see her to say how sorry I was – I felt I had to, really, because she must have known that it was Tony who found Gwen – and she didn't seem terribly distressed. But I couldn't really tell what she was feeling.'

We reached the gate of Tithings Cottage at the same time as two other ladies, and there was a little polite shuffle in the doorway and a murmured conversation about nothing in particular as we went in.

Inside I had a general impression of exposed beams and open fireplaces with bread ovens. There was a great deal of heavy carved oak furniture and the windows were very small with lattice panes that obscured most of the light. Betty introduced me to Molly Richmond. She was a tall, comfortable-looking woman. Not fat but – to use an old-fashioned word – buxom. Her long grey hair was insecurely caught up on top of her head and there was a cheerful smile on her round face. She looked for all the world like Mrs Bun the Baker's Wife in my old set of Happy Families.

'I'm glad Betty brought you along,' she said and I was startled by her voice, which was deep and rather beautiful. 'We must try and have a chat later, when the crowd has dispersed! Meanwhile do go and find a cup of coffee.'

The cottage was quite full and rather too many people were crowded into the two downstairs rooms that were in use. Coffee was being served in the sitting room and there was a table set out with jars of marmalade, cakes and potted plants in the dining room. I took advantage of the crush to have a really good look round. As I always do I looked first at the bookshelves. Quite a few of the books were classical texts or proceedings of archaeological societies and I imagined that they had belonged to Gwen. Those about birds and wildlife I took to be Molly's along with some really splendid Phaidon Press art books. There were a lot of framed photographs too. I identified a middle-aged clergyman (quite High Church, I deduced from the height of his collar) as their father and decided that the handsome woman in an early-1920s coat and skirt must have been their mother. There were several photographs of the two girls as young children and one of Molly as a jolly schoolgirl wearing a gymslip with the waistline down around her hips. Gwen had obviously been the pretty one – small and slim with dark hair and very beautiful large dark eyes. There were photographs of her at all ages – in her late teens with her hair down her back, a wartime one, dressed as a land girl with short hair under the rather becoming hat, one standing among classical ruins in Greece, others by a Bernini fountain in Rome and by the Duomo in Florence. Always with her head held high, gazing directly at the camera as if issuing a challenge. There was a fairly recent one, taken outside the cottage, and although the hair was now grey the dark eyes were still as commanding as ever.

The morning progressed as all coffee mornings do. I bought a ginger cake and Betty bought a jar of marmalade. The headmistress of the village school (looking, as Betty and I decided later, unbelievably young to be a headmistress) spoke briefly about the work of the school and urged us to give generously to the cause. Eventually other women (there were only a couple of middle-aged men, obviously retired and brought along by their wives) drifted away and only Betty and I were left. I seized my chance.

'Now you *must* let us help you do the washing up,' I said, gathering up a couple of cups and heading resolutely towards the kitchen.

It was a good, old-fashioned kitchen with an ancient Aga, a large wooden table and cupboards and open shelves rather than fancy units. Betty, as she usually did, took charge.

'I'll wash, Sheila can wipe, and will you put away, Molly, because you know where everything goes.'

I picked up a drying-up cloth with a picture of Leeds Castle on it and said to Molly, 'It was very well attended wasn't it? How much do you think you will have made?'

'Alison Notley, who is our treasurer, thinks we may have cleared sixty-five pounds.'

We talked about the work of the school and the village in general.

'It's really changed quite a bit, hasn't it,' I said. 'Just in the last five years or so. All those houses beyond the Falkland Arms, done up and rethatched. And new building too.'

'Time stood still here for a couple of hundred years, but I'm afraid it was too good to last – the old cottages were gentrified and the village will never be the same again. Gwen could hardly believe it when she came back.'

'She'd been away for a long time?'

'Most of her life. She went abroad just after the war – she was with the British Council you know – first to Italy and then to Greece. I didn't really think she'd ever live in England again. She came back once in the sixties and worked at the Bodleian for a year, but she couldn't settle and so she went out to the British School in Athens to work in the library there. I think she only came back last year because of some disagreement with the new director. I never fathomed the ins and outs of it all.'

'She was lucky to be able to come back and live with you – and in such a lovely cottage.'

'I didn't, actually, have much choice. She simply turned up one day, right out of the blue, and announced that she'd come home. It's true that Mother left us the cottage jointly, but I never expected to share it with Gwen.'

She turned and put a stack of saucers into one of the cupboards so that I couldn't see her face, but I had the impression that she was frowning.

'One does get set in one's ways if one lives alone,' I said. 'I know I've found that.'

'Gwen was – how shall I put it? – rather domineering. She tended to take people over. Even though she was two years younger than me.'

'Oh, don't talk to me about younger sisters!' Betty exclaimed. 'Gillian's the absolute limit! No one can get a word in edgeways when she's around!'

'But it must have been a dreadful shock – the accident, I mean. It must have upset you dreadfully.'

In the cosy domestic intimacy of the kitchen I didn't feel too awkward about introducing such a delicate subject. Molly was silent for a moment, as if she'd never actually considered the question before. Then she said, 'The accident, yes. Any fatal accident is always shocking. But, no, I didn't feel upset. She'd been away for so long, it was like something happening to a stranger. And, if I'm honest, I didn't really like her much anyway. When we were children I actually hated her.'

She paused and stood quite still, a milk jug in her hands. Then she smiled.

'Isn't that shocking! It's something I don't think I've ever admitted to myself before!' She put the jug on the table. 'But it's true. She was my parents' favourite. She was tiny and lively and pretty and good at games as well. The parents were absolutely mad about golf – we used to go on golfing holidays, it was quite dreadful. I was fat and slow and useless! I used to go off with a sketching pad . . . Gwen was very bright – she went up to Oxford and read Greats. They wouldn't let me go to London to the Slade – I was offered a place, but they didn't think it was *suitable* for their daughter. So I stayed in Banbury, which is where we lived, and kept house for them until my father died and then my mother was left this cottage by an aunt, so then I came and kept house here. She died eight years ago. She was a great age, everyone said. Gwen didn't come back for the funeral. But Mother left the cottage to her as well as to me . . . '

Her voice died away. Then she said briskly, 'Look, it's nearly lunchtime. Do stay and have a bowl of soup. Let's have a glass of sherry first – I think we've earned one!'

We moved back to the sitting room and as Molly took a bottle and some glasses from the oak dresser, I said, 'I wonder, do you mind if I pop up to the bathroom?'

'Of course – it's at the top of the stairs, on the right.'

All the doors upstairs were open. I decided that the room at the front of the house was Molly's bedroom. It was more of a study than a bedroom, with bookshelves all round the walls and a desk in the window, to catch what light there was. There were books and papers everywhere. Obviously Molly was not of the school that tidies everything away when people are coming. I wished that I had her strength of mind. There was a small room that contained an easel and a work table, which was presumably where she did her painting and the third room must have been Gwen's. It was very tidy, compared with the other two rooms. The bed was made up with a smooth, white honeycomb bedspread and there was a wardrobe and a dressing table, set out with silver-backed brushes and an old-fashioned ring-tree. There was also a small table beside the bed with two framed photographs. I listened to the murmur of voices downstairs to make sure that Molly was safely engaged in conversation, and then slipped quickly into the room. One photograph showed Gwen, in her twenties with her arm round the shoulder of a young man. He was about the same age, very good looking in a delicate, rather feminine way. They were standing in the ruins of a small, ancient amphitheatre with wild flowers at their feet. The other photograph was a formal studio portrait of the same young man. The head was in profile, like an idealised head on an ancient coin and this larger study emphasised the fine line of the jaw and the cheekbones. I wondered who he was.

When I returned to the sitting room Betty said, 'I've just been telling Molly about the article you're doing now.'

'It seems strange,' Molly said, 'that the novels we read, just as books, should now be the subject of learned studies!'

'Time does rush by,' I said. 'Before you know where you are life has become history.'

'It's wartime writers you are dealing with, I believe?'

'Yes. It's maddening, really. I feel very conscious of my lack of background. I was born just before the war so I wasn't old enough to remember very much. I've done some background *reading*, of course, as well as the novels, but I still don't quite have the *feel* of the period, if you know what I mean. Were you here during the war or in Banbury?'

'I was stuck in Banbury with Mother – I worked at the local hospital, that was my war work. Gwen had to be off and away. She did some driving in the FANYs for a bit and then – I can't imagine why – she joined the Land Army. She was on a farm near Kidlington, but I don't think she enjoyed it much, though she would never admit that she'd made the wrong decision about anything! Anyway, in 1944 she transferred to the WAAF and went up to Scotland. She had a much livelier war than I did!'

Molly moved a pile of gardening magazines from the small table at her side and put down her sherry glass.

'Come to think of it,' she said, 'Gwen kept a diary for part of the war – though she didn't keep it up for long. I came across it the other day when I was clearing her things out. It might have some useful background stuff if you'd like to have a look at it. I'll find it and send it on to you.'

'That is really very kind of you – I'm sure it would be most useful. You get a real sense of immediacy from a diary – it makes it all so vivid. I'll take great care of it and let you have it back as soon as I've read it.'

'Oh, don't bother. I don't want it back. As I said, Gwen meant very little to me by the end.'

After we had had some excellent lentil soup and apple tart Betty hustled us away. Molly came to the door to say goodbye.

'I won't forget about the diary,' she said. 'I really want to have a good clear-out so that I can turn that room back into a proper studio again, as it used to be before she came back.'

Betty talked non-stop on the way back about the Great Tew village school and the preservation of rural England, expecting no more than an interested murmur from me. I was glad not to have to make conversation because I had a lot to think about. Was Molly quite indifferent about her sister, or had she felt more deeply the unfairness of her own life and fury at the casual way Gwen had come back to interrupt the first independence and real happiness that Molly had ever known. She seemed placid enough, but I knew that women of her generation especially had learned to hide their deeper, rawer feelings behind a mask of politeness and conventional behaviour. It would not have been surprising if a bitter resentment had festered over the years. I knew too that family hatreds were often the strongest of all. I found myself wondering if Molly ever read in the Bodleian, and where she had been on the day that Gwen had died. I was annoyed with myself for having missed the chance of asking her. I would somehow have to make another opportunity of seeing her.

It was well on into the afternoon when we got back and it hardly seemed worth going into Oxford so I thought I might help Betty put leaflets into envelopes and type out the agenda for one of her meetings. I was wrestling with Betty's old portable typewriter, which had the nasty habit of working its way to the edge of the table as one hit the keys, when the telephone rang. It was Fitz, inviting me to dinner the following evening.

'I have also invited Professor Howard – I believe you said you had met him – to make up the numbers. I trust that is agreeable to you? Quite informal. We will expect you at seven for seven-thirty, then.'

I went back to my typing feeling very cheerful. It would be lovely to dine (one used the word instinctively in this context) with Fitz and Elaine – and very pleasant to see Chester Howard again. I began to plan what I would wear. My black blouse would be all right, but I had been meaning to buy a new skirt – something a bit fancier than the winter ones I had with me – perhaps I might just slip into Marks and Spencer tomorrow and see what they had.

I finished the typing and said to Betty, 'If you don't mind, I'll just go up and wash my hair.'

The next day was brilliantly sunny but with a few dark clouds racing across the sky – a typical April day in fact. An 'Oh, to be in England!' sort of day, I thought happily as I walked across the Parks, my thoughts of Fitz leading to Browning.

Pamela now greeted me as an old friend, which was nice, and I settled down comfortably to work. I was disturbed, however, by a pile of folders crashing down beside me on to the desk and an agitated voice saying, 'Oh, I am sorry – they slipped out of my hand – I'm so sorry to have disturbed you.'

Other readers around us raised their heads in enquiry or irritation.

'That's quite all right,' I said, bending down to rescue some papers that had slid to the floor. 'Here you are.'

'Thank you so much. Is anyone sitting here?'

She was a woman in her forties, of medium height and rather stocky. A pair of dark-rimmed spectacles, which were resting half-way down her nose, dominated a nondescript face. She seemed very disorganised and stuffed the papers back into her files in no sort of order and dropped her pencil on to the floor.

'Blast!' she said and went to the desk to use the pencil sharpener.

Tony brought her a heavy volume and she settled down to work. She was up again almost immediately and back at the desk. I heard her say in an agitated voice, 'Oh dear – I seem to have filled in the slip all wrong. I wanted

the article on pendant semi-circle scyphoe. It's in the BSA
– British School in Athens – '82 and this is BSA
'81. I'm *so* sorry.'

'That's all right,' Tony said soothingly. 'Just sit down
and I'll get it for you.'

The woman came back and sat down. But it was difficult
to concentrate on my work because she was scrabbling
about among her papers and making little muttered comments to herself as she did so. I had instinctively reacted
when I heard her asking for the Proceedings of the British
School in Athens, but, of course, there was no reason why
there should be any connection. She only seemed to want
to verify some references and didn't stay long. When she
had gone I went over to Tony and asked who she was.

'That's Dr Lassiter. She works in the Heberden Room
at the Ashmolean – old coins. Strictly speaking all those
BSA proceedings shouldn't be here; I've had to get them
over for her on the conveyor . . . '

The telephone went and he moved away to answer
it before I could ask him anything about Dr Lassiter,
whose name sounded somehow familiar. I went back to
my desk worrying away at it, but it was only as I retrieved
my umbrella from George at lunchtime that I remembered
that it was he who had mentioned her as one of the people
who had been working in Room 45 on the day that Gwen
Richmond had died.

I was musing on this as I pushed my way round
a crowded Marks and Spencer, but all thoughts of Dr
Lassiter, and Gwen Richmond for that matter, went
right out of my head when I found just the skirt I'd been
looking for. It was very full, with a large paisley pattern
in terracotta, stone and olive green on a black background. Miraculously they had it in my size and the right
length and, inspired by this, I also bought myself a new lipstick in a clear bright coral – the sort of colour I thought
I had given up wearing years ago.

I left the Bodleian early to give myself plenty of

time to change. As I stood in front of the mirror curling the back of my hair with my electric tongs it occurred to me that the wheel had really come full circle and that I was once again wearing the same hairstyle (it used to be called a page-boy bob) that I had had when I first met Rupert and Fitz, though what, if any, significance this had I really couldn't imagine. I gave myself a little shake to dispel the ghosts of the past and decided to concentrate on the present.

I considered Dr Lassiter as a suspect. If she *had* been in Room 45 on the day of Gwen's death, it would have been easy for her to slip away, commit the crime and then come back half an hour later. I knew from my own experience that when you were working you were more or less oblivious of the comings and goings around you. And Tony, Pamela and Felicity were usually too busy at their desks each end of the room to check on the movements of the readers.

In the corridors she would have been an unobtrusive figure, in her natural setting, you might say, a perfect camouflage. She was quite sturdy – she could easily have brought a heavy book down on Gwen's head, especially if, as seemed likely, Gwen had been sitting down, and a handbag would easily hold quite a large screwdriver. As for motive – well – I thought suddenly of *Gaudy Night* and the motive there – something to do with research, perhaps? If they had both been in Greece, Gwen could easily have found out that Dr Lassiter had suppressed some vital ancient document to fit a thesis or had plagiarised something – there were all sorts of scholarly crimes that Dr Lassiter might have been guilty of and that Gwen knew about. I became quite excited about my theory and it was only when the tongs slipped and burned my neck that I realised that now I would have to hurry if I wasn't to be unforgivably late.

Chapter Eight

Fortunately the traffic *into* Oxford in the evenings is relatively light and I arrived in Norham Gardens quite early and was able to park a few doors away from Fitz's house where I sat in the car for ten minutes listening to *The Archers* on the radio, then put on a final dab of face powder and presented myself on the doorstep a fashionable five minutes late, as Rupert used to say.

I was glad of the reassurance of my new skirt since Fitz was wearing a dark brown velvet jacket and Chester Howard, who was already there and had risen politely from his chair as I entered, was wearing a dark suit and bow tie which, with his white shirt, looked almost like evening dress.

Fitz seated me in a triangular chair upholstered in slippery straw-coloured satin and wondered what I would like to drink.

'That delicious Sercial would be lovely,' I said.

'If you wish,' he said. 'Unless you would care to be more *adventurous*, as it were. We seem to be drinking ouzo.'

He raised a glass full of an opalescent milky liquid, clinking pleasantly with ice.

'I think that might be a little strong for me,' I replied, 'since I'm driving. Perhaps I could have some vermouth.'

'Ah.' Fitz considered this with some care. 'Shall we give you French vermouth or Italian . . . or perhaps – I know – you shall have some Punt e Mes!'

I caught Chester Howard's eye and we both smiled as Fitz poured out a brownish-coloured drink, which I discovered to my dismay tasted rather like cough medicine.

'How is Benson progressing, Professor Howard?' I asked.

'My friends call me Bill,' he said, 'and Benson is doing very nicely thank you. The Bodleian is full of unexpected treasures. I found a letter from Ivor Novello, the other day – isn't that marvellous? – about a dramatisation of *Mapp and Lucia* that Benson had done – now wouldn't *that* have been something!'

We chatted about his work for a while and then I asked Fitz about Elaine.

'She is in the kitchen unmoulding the avocado mousse – always an anxious moment, don't you find? Will it come away cleanly? Will the whole thing, indeed, collapse, as it did on one memorable occasion some years ago when I served it to Robert Frost.'

Elaine had always been a brilliant cook, but I hadn't known of Fitz's interest in cooking.

'It was *America* that made me into a cook, my dear Chloe. Restaurant food in the United States is (with a few exceptions) not edible – *not* the sort of thing one could consider offering to one's guests, so I was obliged to learn the rudiments of the culinary art. Like most things it is not difficult if one applies intelligence and concentration. It is, however, perfectly possible to eat very well in American homes.' He made a little bow in Bill's direction.

'Forgive me,' Bill said, 'I thought your name was Sheila, but Fitz calls you Chloe?'

'Oh, that is a joke from long ago,' I said. 'But, come to think of it, we are none of us using our given names tonight – I am Chloe instead of Sheila, you are Bill and not Chester and Fitz— '

'Yes my dear,' he broke in irritably, 'we all know what *my* given name is.'

'Do you think,' I suggested frivolously, 'that it means we are all three hiding behind aliases, like masks, concealing our true natures?'

'I do not believe,' Fitz said meditatively, 'that I remember any more *what* my true nature is.'

'Perhaps we are only truly ourselves in our extreme youth,' Bill suggested, 'and become less ourselves as we react to other people.'

'All life is subjective – indeed, metaphysical. Do we in fact exist at all?'

'Superficial chat about life and metaphysics, Chloe dear, went out with undergraduate cocoa parties in the nineteen thirties,' Fitz said sternly. 'Let me give you another drink.'

'No, thank you, I'm fine.' I indicated my almost untouched glass.

As he was pouring drinks for Bill and for himself, Elaine came into the room. Like the house and like her brother she too had hardly changed. When I had first known her she was in early middle age and had already set the style of her appearance. She too was tall and still moved gracefully. Her long face, with large eyes and delicate features, and the way her hair was caught up into a knot behind reminded me, as it always had, of Virginia Woolf. She had always worn 'artistic' clothes – long skirts and kerchiefs, like Augustus John's women – and this evening she had a long full skirt of a subtle russet brown, a pink shirt and a black velvet waistcoat. She looked absolutely splendid. She came towards me holding out both her hands.

'So this is little Chloe! Dear child, how well I remember those grey eyes. You were my Ophelia, don't you remember?'

Indeed, I had forgotten. She had had the habit of making members of Fitz's circle sit for her and I had been Ophelia when she was doing the illustrations for an edition of Lamb's *Tales from Shakespeare*. Not, thank goodness, in a tin bath full of water like poor Lizzie Siddal, though uncomfortable enough, crouched on the ground, dressed in a white robe with scratchy garlands in my hair, clutching a posy of flowers, doing my best to convey madness rather than embarrassment. Rupert, I now remembered, had been a magnificent Mercutio in Elizabethan velvets and satins with a cloak which he was most reluctant to be parted from.

We went into the dining room, Elaine taking with her a large gin and tonic which Fitz declared was the *nadir* of unadventurousness.

As we seated ourselves at the oak refectory table, which would have been quite at home in some mediaeval hall, I saw that the avocado mousse *had* been successfully unmoulded. It was delicious and I complimented Elaine on its delicate flavour and texture. Fitz broke in.

'I was rather *concerned*,' he said, 'whether or not the first and last courses might be too *bland*. I have, myself, made a soufflée for our last course – sadly we no longer observe the custom of having a savoury – and I feared that there might not be enough *contrast* of textures. However, we decided to have a really sturdy *roast* for the main dish, so I do believe that the balance has, on the whole, been properly preserved.'

He and Bill then embarked antiphonally on a long and detailed anecdote about a particularly memorable meal they had eaten somewhere in France, which involved an Italian count, a stolen goose and some white truffles. I noted that Fitz and Bill had been on holiday in France together. As I listened to their conversation, which was elliptical and full of allusions, I noted an ease and intimacy – a *familiarity* (though that was not a word I would ever have expected to use of Fitz) that indicated that there was, or had been, something more than friendship between them. I decided ruefully that I need not have bothered to buy a new skirt. When Bill said that he no longer had a family, he had not been referring to a wife

and children. I blushed inwardly at my own naïvety –
that would teach me to have foolish and uncharacteristic
thoughts at my age!

I recovered myself to find that Elaine was asking
me about Michael.

'I gather from Arthur' – she still resolutely called
her brother by his correct name – 'that you have a
son up at Oxford. It so happens that I am making a
few studies for a children's book on the Round Table
and I badly need a model for Sir Mordred. Is he, by any
chance, *dark*?'

I thought of Michael's reaction to such a proposal
and said hastily, 'Well, no, actually, he's sort of fairish
brown, rather like me . . . '

'Is he? Then he *might* just do for Sir Perceval.'

'And,' I went on, 'he's rather tied up at the moment,
with Schools, you know. It's his last term.'

'Always an anxious time,' Bill said.

I found that I was now able to meet his eye and
said, 'Almost more anxious for the poor parents! The
young seem amazingly casual about such things – though
perhaps they simply don't want us to know what they are
feeling.'

'So many of them,' he replied, 'at least in my experience, retreat into a sort of dumbness – I use the word in
both its English and American senses. It is not that they
are inarticulate, but they just can't seem to be bothered
to communicate verbally with anyone.'

'In my day,' I said, 'we hid behind a great cloud of
verbiage – usually frivolous – perhaps *that's* what they
lack, frivolity!'

'The use of words,' Fitz announced, 'or, indeed, the
non-use of words, as Bill has said, as a means of expressing, or not expressing, thoughts or emotions is, after all,
one of man's main achievements, one, I need hardly add,
that separates us from the lower animals.'

We considered this in silence for a moment and then

Bill said, 'The number of words, however, does not necessarily relate to the clarity of expression. Think of Henry James.'

'Oh yes,' I broke in. 'Like when he described a black dog as "something dark, something canine"!'

'That seems perfectly reasonable to me,' Fitz said, 'admirably lucid.'

'Surely that's not the first word one thinks of in relation to James – after all he, himself, refers to his "sub-aqueous prose".'

'It is the *thought* behind the prose that is lucid, my dear Chloe,' Fitz explained patiently, 'not necessarily the words themselves.'

Elaine brought in a splendid rib of beef which Fitz carved expertly. I watched him carefully. When I carve, however much I study the little diagrams in the cookery books, the joint always seems to fall apart and I end up with a few ragged slices and lots of little bits.

The meal progressed on its stately way and the conversation became more intellectually strenuous. I felt I had become rather out of practice. Dinner-party chat (one cannot really dignify it by the name of conversation) in Taviscombe mostly consists of gossip, frequently expressed worries about our children and speculation as to why petrol should cost so much more in our part of the West Country than it does anywhere else. Not much to exercise what now passes for my mind. I began to feel rather tired and was quite glad, after the meal was over, to sink into a peaceful silence while Fitz embarked on the ritual of making Turkish coffee. Actually it always seems to me an awful lot of fuss about nothing, since what you end up with is, in my opinion, nothing more or less than lukewarm mud. Still, I hoped its excessive strongness would help to keep me awake. I suppose it's a sign of advancing age, but I do find it difficult to keep my eyelids from drooping after a heavy meal in the evening. Finally the contents of the curiously shaped brass coffee jug were pronounced ready to drink and conversation could become more general. I started to tell Elaine how much I had always admired her book illustrations.

'I bought all your editions for Michael when he was a child. He still loves them, especially your *Arabian Nights*.'

She blushed, unexpectedly, with pleasure.

'Perhaps you might like to have a look at my *Round Table* ones?' she asked tentatively.

'Oh yes, please, that would be marvellous!'

She got to her feet and I willingly abandoned my cup of Turkish mud and followed her up the splendid staircase, whose walls were hung with large oil paintings after the school of Alma Tadema, to her studio at the front of the house.

It was a large room, finely proportioned and with a high, noble ceiling, decorated with intricate plasterwork which featured heads of cherubs picked out in gold. The whole walls were hung with a profusion of pictures, mostly the framed originals of Elaine's illustrations. I recognised Michael's favourite – 'The Djinn', all sinuous coils, emerging from a jewel-encrusted bottle. There was a background of columns and rich hangings, and, through an archway, a glimpse of a magically beautiful garden. I remembered how, as a small child, he had been torn between fear at the idea of the Djinn and delight in the beauty of the picture. The strength of Elaine's illustrations was that she never sentimentalised her subject – the fear was always there as well as the beauty. In spite of her surroundings, her Arthurian studies owed nothing to Burne-Jones. She had evolved a new technique with light and heavy ink lines defining the delicate water-colour figures, so that the character of each person came startlingly to life.

'How do you like my Merlin?' she asked, turning an easel towards me.

A magnificent figure in heavy robes was standing in one

of Fitz's most characteristic poses – his head thrown back, so that the thick hair was shaken off the brow and the right hand raised in benediction. The expression was one I had often seen, an expression that conveyed a supreme confidence in his own values and opinions – Fitz the infallible.

'Oh yes, I'm sure that Merlin was *exactly* like Fitz!' I exclaimed. 'How clever of you!'

She smiled and showed me some of the other studies. Arthur and Guinevere, although delightfully done, somehow didn't have the life and vitality of Merlin, rather as though she had been bored by them.

'Where is Lancelot?' I asked. 'Have you done him yet?'

'He's in my bedroom. I always put pictures I'm not quite sure about where I can see them first thing, when I wake up. I find that helps me to decide what is wrong with them.'

'May I see?'

She opened a door that led out of the studio and put on the light. My first reaction was pleasure that Elaine slept in a four-poster bed, just like the princesses in her fairy tales. My second reaction was amazement, for on a table beside the four-poster bed was a framed photograph of a young man. It was the same photograph that I had seen beside Gwen Richmond's bed. I gave an involuntary cry of astonishment and went to look at it more closely. Elaine looked at me enquiringly.

'What an amazingly beautiful young man.' I said. 'Who is he?'

She picked up the photograph and cradled it in her hands.

'That was Lance,' she said, 'my younger brother. You see, I have used him for his namesake – that is why I wanted the picture to be absolutely right.'

The picture on an easel at the foot of the bed was larger than the other studies, not so much an illustration, more a portrait. It was a full-length study of a young man in armour leaning against a may tree in full bloom. His sword and helmet were on the ground, intertwined with briar roses and convolvulus, which had magically sprung up to cover them. His face was raised to look at the flowers above his head and wore such an expression of sadness and despair that I felt I could hardly bear to look at it.

'Oh, Elaine,' I said inadequately.

Rupert had told me that Fitz and Elaine had worshipped their younger brother. Elaine's gift for painting and Fitz's scholarly achievements were both remarkable but Lance had really been the golden boy of that talented family. He had written a novel that was widely acclaimed for both its style and originality, a study of Shelley, still considered a classic, and a play that held the promise of great things to come. He had died abroad, a few years after the end of the war and, Rupert said, they had never really got over the tragedy. Looking at the picture I realised that Elaine's grief at his death was undiminished by time. At least she was able to express her sorrow through her painting; it must have been much harder for Fitz. I had never once heard him refer to his brother.

There were so many questions I wanted to ask Elaine about Lance and his connection with Gwen Richmond but, with this moment of emotion hanging in the air between us, it would have been crass to do so. I said hesitantly, 'You still miss him very much?'

'There isn't a moment in the day when he isn't in my thoughts.'

'And Fitz?'

'Arthur thinks his own thoughts.'

She stood aside to let me through the door and put out the light carefully, as if extinguishing a flame in front of a shrine.

As I came down the stairs I felt I had been in another world and it seemed astonishing to find Fitz and Bill Howard still drinking coffee and discussing George Eliot. Soon after, I made my excuses and went away, feeling that the evening had been almost *too* eventful.

96

Chapter Nine

Although the following morning was bright and sunny I no longer felt the same euphoria I had known the day before as I walked through the Parks. The flowers and the blossom on the trees seemed almost unbearably beautiful – Housman not Browning, I felt, fitted my mood today. Or Eliot. April is indeed the cruellest month, mixing memory not with desire exactly, but with a kind of indefinable yearning, the restlessness that had led me into foolish thoughts about Bill Howard. Spring is for the young, I told myself sternly, it is the youth of the year. Middle age is autumnal, with the sere and yellow leaf, not the delicate green of unfolding buds, and this feeling of being poised on the edge of some great adventure is unsuitable and unbecoming and will only end in tears.

I settled down to work and managed to lose myself, as mercifully I can, in another, more sober world, not surfacing until nearly half past one. I knew that all the pubs and most of the cafés would be very crowded, so I made my way to a small vegetarian restaurant so tucked away down a side street that only its regular customers know of its existence. Harriet (a born-again Vegan) had discovered it and I'd been there several times with Betty. I noticed gratefully that they'd relaxed their original strict principles because there was a cheese topping on the very good ratatouille.

I opened my book and had just started to eat, when a

voice behind me said, '*Isn't* this a coincidence – I've just been posting a parcel to you!'

It was Molly Richmond. She put her tray down and distributed various dishes around the table.

'How nice to see you,' I said. And, indeed, it really did seem like a heaven-sent opportunity to ask some of the questions that were churning round in my mind.

'I found Gwen's diary,' she said, breaking up bits of bread and stirring them round in her soup. 'I thought there were two of them but I could only find one. Still it should give you some idea of what it was like to live in the countryside in wartime.'

We talked a little about the war and then, when there was a pause in the conversation, I said, 'I had dinner with the Fitzgeralds last night, I believe your sister knew them.'

She stared at me, her face looking particularly large and round across the small table.

'The Fitzgeralds? Elaine and Arthur?'

'Yes.'

'I am very surprised that Gwen's name was mentioned in that household,' she said. Her voice was hard and cold.

'I think *I* may have mentioned her,' I said vaguely. 'Do you know them too?'

'Elaine Fitzgerald was my dearest friend. She was also my teacher. Everything I know about painting I have learnt from her.'

'You say *was*,' I ventured.

'How could I bring myself to face her after the terrible thing that Gwen did to them both.'

There was a moment's silence. I longed to ask the question, but somehow I couldn't.

Then Molly said, 'She killed their brother Lance, who was, as you may know, the light of their lives.'

'*Killed*?'

'As good as. Oh, she didn't stab him with a knife,

98

or poison him or push him over a cliff. She loved him, I believe, in her own peculiar way. But Gwen was, nevertheless, the cause of his death.'

She was sitting quite still, her hands resting on the edge of the table. She began to push some spilt breadcrumbs around with the tip of one finger.

'How did it happen?' I asked.

'It's a long story,' she said. 'I first got to know Elaine Fitzgerald in the last months of the war. She was doing Red Cross work and came to the hospital in Banbury on a course. We found we had a lot in common – though she was older than me. She was already a well-known illustrator and I was still upset at not having been allowed to study art in London – just knowing her was very thrilling for me. She offered to give me lessons, so, whenever I could, I got the bus to Oxford and spent marvellous hours in that studio of hers. The journeys were difficult and tiring (especially when I'd just been on night duty) but they seemed like expeditions into a different world. It was the happiest time of my life. Her brother Arthur was away doing some sort of hush-hush work and Lance was in the Air Force. I saw them from time to time, and they were agreeable to me as Elaine's friend, but I hardly noticed them. All I thought about was Elaine and the work and the atmosphere in that wonderful house.'

'It is still almost unchanged,' I said, then stopped, afraid to break the thread of her narrative. She hardly seemed aware that I had spoken.

'One of the best things for me was being *important* to someone. At home it was always Gwen who came first, and with other people *she* was the popular one. That house was a special place for me, where I could be myself – where my gifts, small as they were, were appreciated and encouraged.

'When Gwen was demobbed she came home for a while. And, of course, as soon as she discovered about my friendship with the Fitzgeralds she wanted to barge in there too. I held out as long as I could, but she could be very persistent, so I asked Elaine if I might bring her with me one day. Gwen could be very charming when she chose. She was lively and intelligent and good company – all the things I was not. Arthur was home by then and he and Elaine took to Gwen and encouraged her to visit them often. I was still working at the hospital so I couldn't get away every week, and Gwen took to going to see them on her own. Before I knew what had happened she was practically part of the household in a way I had never been. Oh, Elaine and I still painted together – but the old atmosphere was gone.'

She broke off and gave me a brief smile.

'I don't know why I'm telling you all this. You're a good listener! I've been bottling it up all these years, and now I've started I don't think I can stop. Do you mind?'

'No, of course not. Please go on.'

'Then Lance came home from the Air Force and I saw at once what Gwen was up to. As soon as she saw him she wanted him. He really was the most beautiful young man – when he was in a room you couldn't look at anyone else. He was brilliant, too, really creative and with a fine mind, and with it all he was shy and modest. He'd had a great success with his novel – everyone said he was the most original writer of his generation. Gwen loved all that, of course – she adored fame and success. Lance, bless him' – her face softened into a smile – 'said he couldn't see what all the fuss was about, he'd just written a book the way he felt like writing it. He had a very sweet nature – he was always so kind and friendly to me . . . Anyway, it was obvious to me that Gwen intended to marry him. But she knew how possessive Elaine and Arthur were. Lance was the most important thing in both their lives. Everything they did was related to him. During the war they'd suffered agonies, being parted from him and worrying about his safety and now

100

that he was back home they lived in a sort of *glow*. Yes,' she said as I looked surprised, 'Arthur as well as Elaine. In some ways he was more obsessed than she was. He was rather different in those days – witty, of course, but a kinder wit and a more generous spirit.

'This all went on for some time – over a year. Gwen was clever. She never betrayed any partiality for Lance – she devoted as much time as ever to Elaine and Arthur, so that they came to think of her as the daughter of the house. They had no idea of her feelings for Lance – she would soon have been turned away if they'd had any inkling.

'Gwen decided that her best chance was to get Lance away from Oxford, away from their influence and protection. She had heard about one of the first archaeological expeditions going into Greece. I don't know if you know what Greece was like in those days. There had been a lot of unrest, partisans fighting and so forth, and it was only just possible to get back into the country. She had a lot of contacts still from her Oxford days and managed to wangle two places for them on the expedition – she was a good classical scholar and he was to write an account of the trip. She was very persuasive and he was wildly excited at the idea of this new and thrilling adventure. I think he was in love with her – though it may just have been that he was overwhelmed by her personality and *thought* he was. The end result was the same – she seemed to have cast a spell over him and he followed wherever she led. Gwen knew that Elaine and Arthur would be horrified if they thought that Lance was going into Greece at that time – it was still quite dangerous – so she persuaded him to keep the whole thing secret. She didn't tell Mother and me anything either, of course. Just that she was going to London to visit friends, and that's what Lance told the Fitzgeralds. The first thing *they* knew about it was a postcard from Lance, posted in Rome, to say that they were on their way to Greece.'

101

'What a cruel thing to do!' I exclaimed.

'Yes. The fact that Lance had kept the whole thing a secret hurt them dreadfully. They sent for me and I was horrified. It was the first I knew about it – Gwen hadn't even bothered to send a postcard to Mother and me. They realised then what sort of person Gwen was and how strong a hold she had over Lance. They blamed me . . . '

Her voice trembled and she was almost in tears.

'But that was so unfair!' I cried.

'Whoever said life was fair?' she said bitterly. 'After a few weeks Mother had a letter from Gwen saying that they were going to investigate a site near Bassae in the Peloponnese. She sounded very pleased with herself, very full of how exciting the work was, how brilliant Lance's book would be. We heard nothing for some time, then I had a letter from Elaine to say that Lance was dead.'

'How terrible – how did he die?'

'It was typhoid. Conditions in those remote parts were very primitive just then, so soon after the war. The water supply was contaminated. Several of the expedition died . . . '

'And Gwen?'

'Oh, Gwen survived. She was a great survivor. She didn't come back to England though. I think I told you she got a job with the British Council and lived abroad.'

'And you never heard from Elaine again?'

'Never. It was as though I no longer existed for her. I don't think anything much existed for her then, apart from her memories of Lance and her painting.'

I thought of Elaine as I had first known her several years after the tragedy. It was true, now I came to think of it, that she hadn't seemed to live in the real world. She only saw Fitz's circle in relation to her pictures – as models or as an audience.

'And Fitz? What about him?'

'I never saw him, of course, but I knew people who knew him – Mother and I had moved to Great Tew by then and I had friends in Oxford – and they said that he had become very sharp and malicious. I think that whereas Elaine had withdrawn into a world of memories and grieving, Arthur's grief was constantly fuelled by anger and bitterness.'

'And Gwen – did she ever see them again?'

'No. She did come back to England briefly – that was when she worked in the Bodleian for a bit – but at that time Elaine never left that house in Norham Gardens and Arthur had gone to Harvard, so you see . . . '

'What a desperately sad story!' I said. 'But is it too late now – now that Gwen is dead – for you to see Elaine again?'

She shook her head. 'Even now, after all these years, I couldn't face her. Her grief for Lance is still strong, I know, and how could she bear to see me . . . '

I remembered Elaine's voice as she spoke of Lance and knew that Molly was right. They could never meet again.

The next morning I woke up feeling terrible. Not a full-blown migraine, thank goodness, but a really awful sick headache. I met Betty on the landing as I was tottering back from the bathroom.

'I'm awfully sorry, but I think I've simply got to stay in bed for a few hours.'

'Oh, poor you! Robert's gone out, but would you like him to look in on you when he gets back?'

'No – it's all right, it's only a headache – you remember how I always used to get them. I'll take my tablets, I've got some with me, and just collapse for a bit.'

'Would you like some tea or anything?'

'No, just water and I've got that. Sorry to be a bore.'

'Don't be ridiculous! Go and lie down!'

I took my tablets and crawled back into bed. It really is

awful being ill away from home, even with your oldest and dearest friends. You feel embarrassed and (even if you're just lying there quietly out of everyone's way) a nuisance. And then, as my friend Rosemary always says, however comfortable any other bed may be it is Your Own Bed that you long for when you're not feeling well.

Some malevolent creature with a sharp instrument was still driving it into my head, just above my left eye and the least movement brought on waves of dizziness and nausea. I tried to lie still and make my mind a blank, but that was impossible. The events of the last few days and all the strange and varied things that I had found out about Gwen Richmond and her sudden death were whirling round in my brain like plunging painted horses on a merry-go-round. All the people she had hurt – Pamela, Molly, Elaine, Fitz – and heaven knows how many others. She had been a woman who wanted her own way and didn't care who she trampled underfoot to get it. And how cruel she was – playing at God with people's lives, getting enjoyment out of tormenting them. I know that the world is full of wickedness and cruelty, goodness knows you can't watch the television news for a single evening without being aware of man's infinite inhumanity to man, but I always find the idea that anyone, especially a woman, can deliberately plan viciousness very shocking.

In the darkness behind my closed and throbbing eyes the faces of Gwen's victims came and went: Molly, whose happiness had been snatched away – so unfairly – for ever by her sister's selfishness; poor little Pamela, driven almost to distraction by her tormentor; Elaine, shut away in a place of sorrow; Fitz, withdrawn to God knows what state of anger and bitterness; and Lance, dead long ago, in a distant country, but still so alive in the minds of three people. How glad they all must be that she was dead, and how terrible that they should feel that way.

104

I was quite sure now that Gwen Richmond had been murdered. All the small things that Tony had noticed about her death had made me feel that it was a possibility, and now I knew what sort of person she was, I was convinced that it must be so. If I was so certain that it was murder and not an accident, should I go to the police and tell them what I had worked out. There was no real *reason* why they should take me seriously. They had made their own investigation and found no suspicious circumstances. I had no evidence of any kind. I imagined trying to explain Fitz or Elaine, or even Molly, to some polite but disbelieving police sergeant. Anyway, an investigation might well uncover Pamela's crime and I certainly didn't want that. In fact, if I thought about it, I didn't really want anyone to suffer for the death of a woman I had come to loathe.

My mouth was very dry and I kept yawning – a sure sign that the tablets were working. I reached out and took a sip of water, but the effort made me feel very dizzy and peculiar. It wasn't right, though, I told myself, as I tried to ease my throbbing head back into the hollow I had made for it in the pillow, it wasn't *right* that murder, however justified, should remain unpunished.

Perhaps I could find out who had killed her. Someone must. But not the police. I would do it. Justice must not just be done, but must be *seen* to be done . . . An eye for an eye . . . Lance and Gwen . . . Lancelot and Guinevere . . . The tablets finally had their effect and I fell asleep.

I was awakened several hours later by Cleopatra jumping on to the bed and sitting heavily on my chest. Fortunately I was feeling much better and it seemed a very pleasant thing to do, simply to lie there, feeling relaxed and rather light-headed (as I usually did after the headache had gone) listening to Cleopatra's vibrant purr and looking into her pale golden eyes which were staring at me with unusual approval. Cats love people to be ill in bed – a captive lap (or chest) that doesn't suddenly get up and go away. Having decided that she had subdued me sufficiently, Cleopatra got up, arched her back, gave a couple of wails by way of conversation, and dived down into the bed where she lay across my feet like a divinely furry hot-water bottle.

My mind was clearer now and the confused thoughts and pictures had gone, but one thing did remain and that was the decision to see what I could find out about Gwen Richmond's death. This was not, I now admitted to myself, out of any burning desire for justice, but simple curiosity. I cannot bear not to know what happens next. This probably explains my passion (deplored by my more serious-minded friends) for radio and television soap operas. I have to ferret away to find explanations for things – quite often things that do not concern me personally at all.

Tony would help, perhaps. I decided that he, too, would want to know what had really happened. I must tell him what I had found out about people's possible motives and see if he agreed with my conclusions. Certainly he could tell me who had been in Room 45 that afternoon and I would somehow have to find out where my three suspects had been at that time. I was sure I could find some excuse for going to see Molly – of *course*, I could return the diary when I had read it. The diary – that should be interesting and would certainly tell me more about Gwen herself. I cast about in my mind for some excuse for seeing Fitz and Elaine again so soon after their dinner party. I had, of course, sent a polite thank-you note to Elaine, but now it occurred to me that I might return their hospitality. It would have to be in a restaurant – I wondered which, if any, of the more expensive Oxford restaurants Fitz might approve of. I could ask Bill Howard, I supposed; he would be certain to know such things. Though if I did I would have to invite him too. Which would make up the numbers as Fitz would say . . . Musing on the relative merits of Italian, Chinese and *nouvelle cuisine* I drifted off to sleep again.

Chapter Ten

The package containing Gwen Richmond's diary was waiting for me when I got up. After a few anxious enquiries about my state of health, Betty had gone out to a meeting and so I had the house to myself and could start reading the diary straight away. It had been written in a notebook with hard covers and I was glad to see that the handwriting was clear and legible. The entries were rather sporadic – it wasn't really a diary as such, but a series of thoughts and impressions. Mostly there weren't even proper dates, but just the days of the week. Well, I told myself, even if it doesn't help me find out anything relevant to Gwen Richmond's murder, at least it will count as research. I began to read with interest and anticipation.

Tuesday. Arrived (on the back of a lorry full of milk-churns!) this afternoon and was plunged straight into milking. Not a bad herd (Herefords) and the milking shed reasonably up to date. The farmer, whose name is Brown, seems a bit disconcerted to have an 'educated' land girl and doesn't seem happy about giving orders to someone of a different class. He's a silent sort of man, I'm glad to say – I don't think I could stand a lot of rural chat! There's a wife and one daughter, both of whom work on the farm. The wife is subdued but appears friendly enough, and the daughter, May, is a pretty girl, who looks as

108

if she might have a bit of the devil in her. They obviously both dote on her. The farmhouse isn't too primitive, thank God, and the kitchen where we all live, is quite warm thanks to a big iron range which is where Mrs B. does the cooking. Thank goodness it's a small farm and I'm the only land girl so I can live in and don't have to be in one of those dreadful hostels with swarms of other girls. For one awful moment I was afraid that I would have to share with the daughter, because Mrs B. said, 'We've put you in May's room' but, mercifully, what they've done is give me the daughter's room while she goes up into the attic or somewhere. It's not bad – a bit poky and very cold – I shall have to ask for another blanket. Still I suppose it could be worse and almost anything is better than being in the forces or in some vile factory.

Saturday. Haven't had time to write anything until today – free until milking this afternoon. I'm dead tired although I haven't done more than go through the motions of learning what's what. Mr B. and I do the milking, turn and turn about, Mrs B. sees to the hens and other odd jobs, May and I are dogsbodies who have to turn our hands to anything. As well as one land girl (me) Mr B. has been allocated one Italian prisoner of war three days a week, to help with the heavier work – ploughing, fencing and so on. His name is Dino and he is delivered from the camp a few miles away by lorry in the morning and taken back at night. He seems a bit full of himself for a prisoner – I may have to take him down a peg or two.

Wednesday. Thank goodness! My Wellington boots arrived today – it was foul having to muck out the cows in my boots and canvas gaiters, I'm sure I'm getting chilblains. Mr B. said the boots would have to last me two years and that I was very lucky to get them – they're only supplied to dairy workers! He must have seen the expression on my face because I could feel that for two pins he'd say, 'Don't you know there's a war on.'

Friday. It's been bitterly cold and wet and I've been grateful for my heavy corduroy breeches. May doesn't seem to feel the cold and was out feeding the pigs today wearing a blouse and skirt and just a thin cotton mac. Thank God for Mrs B.'s stove to dry out my heavy socks and pullovers. I've been reduced to draping myself in old sacks in this rain, but nothing ever seems to get properly dry. We've been carting muck for the last two days and I don't think I'll ever get used to the all-pervading smell. Insult to injury! After deducting for my board and lodgings, I was left with only 22s 6d of my weekly pay! I suppose I'm lucky that at least I get properly fed – Mrs B.'s a decent cook – some of the girls I met in Oxford last week were telling me that they're half starved most of the time.

Tuesday. May seems to have taken a fancy to me. She asked if I had thought of going to a dance at the airfield this weekend. Apparently she goes every week. I don't think her parents are very happy about it, but she can wind them around her little finger. I can't say the idea appeals to me, but I suppose it can't be worse than sitting in that kitchen with the Browns, listening to dreadful comedy programmes, or stuck up in my freezing room trying to read by the light of a bedside lamp, the shade so covered with frills (May's choice) that hardly any light gets out!

Sunday. Well, we got to the dance. May all done up in a pink angora jumper, short tight skirt and high heels and me in the only frock I've got with me. We went on our bicycles – it isn't very pleasant trying to cycle in the blackout with these dim lamps and I nearly went into a ditch several times. I was right about May – she is quite flighty, she was surrounded by airmen all cutting in in the 'excuse me' dances. It was all a bit dreary really, but at least they had some drink, which is almost impossible to get in the village. I found a sergeant who wanted to drink rather than dance and passed the time listening to him maundering on about his wife and children!

Monday. Dino brought along another Italian prisoner today to help with the muck-spreading. I think they're up to something. I was moving some bales of feed in the yard when they came in to load up the tractor and they didn't know I was there. My Italian's a bit rusty but from what I could gather there's some sort of racket going on – something to do with the airfield and supplies going missing from there. I couldn't discover if Mr B. was involved but it wouldn't surprise me – I think he's certainly got an eye to the main chance. I don't know quite how the Italians are involved – I think they're the middle-men – Italian entrepreneurial talent! Certainly they seem quite free to move about the countryside. Dino, for instance, goes up to the airfield twice a week to collect the pig swill for Mr B. It's a job I should do really, because I'm better with the horses than he is, but I can see now why he's so keen to do it. I thought from the beginning that our Dino was a bit shifty – he's a cocky little brute – I must see if I can find out what's going on.

Saturday. Another dance at the airfield. May spent the whole of yesterday evening putting her hair up in hundreds of little pin curls which she kept in all day today under a turban. Her face was plastered with make-up – I don't know how she gets hold of it – I haven't seen a lipstick for months! At the dance she disappeared for a couple of hours and only turned up just when the band was playing the National Anthem. That young lady will have to look out or she'll end up in trouble! My bike pump has gone again. I swear it's that blasted Italian. I confronted him last time it went missing and he denied it – so I threatened to tell Mr B. and lo and behold it suddenly appeared again in my bicycle basket!

Monday. Back after a few days leave. Mother and Molly don't know they're born! Molly moans away about night duty at the hospital and Mother is always complaining about the rations – honestly, they ought to try living in this vile place. Still it was nice to have a proper bath again and wear some decent clothes and get some sleep – I simply stayed in bed one day, didn't get up at all! It all seems more hellish here when you've been away. May says she's missed me. I think she missed having someone to confide in. Not that she's got much of interest to say. She really is a very stupid girl – a typical dumb blonde with her head full of young men and clothes and cinema actors. She said she'd seen *The Man in Grey* four times. When we have a free afternoon I sometimes go with her to the cinema. But it's always pretty awful getting into Oxford. There are so few buses and always crowded. Last week it was so full coming back that people were sitting on the stairs. It seems odd to be in Oxford these days. Some of the colleges are full of evacuated ministries and the place is swarming with 'refugees' from London – it's all pretty horrible. Still, it seems like heaven after this place – civilisation!

Friday. I had to go into the village this afternoon to deliver some carrots to Mrs Price at the shop. She still hasn't got any U2 torch batteries but I did manage to get a flat one for my rear light. I came home along the back lane. As I came round the corner by the Hanger wood I saw our cart and old Royal grazing by the roadside. No sign of Dino. I had just got off my bike to investigate when he emerged from the deep ditch. He didn't see me and got back into the cart and drove off. When he was out of sight I went to investigate. In the ditch were two large jerry cans full of petrol. So that's what he's up to!

Thursday. Still keeping an eye on Dino and making a few innocent enquiries in the village. There seems to be quite a flourishing little black market going on. Tinned food, drink, cigarettes – as well as the petrol, presumably. The other Italian, Luigi, is coming tomorrow so I must see if I can eavesdrop again.

Friday. I was wrong about Mr B. being in this racket – I think he buys the occasional bottle of whisky under the counter, but that's all – so Dino is very anxious he doesn't find out. I was able to listen in to the Italians' conversation quite easily because I managed to get up into the hayloft while they were working down below. It really is very highly organised – several people in the village are in on it – especially Ray Burton at the garage – and they seem to have contacts in several villages all round. Talk about the Mafia!

Tuesday. I wonder which of the men at the airfield are doing the stealing. I hope it isn't any of May's boyfriends. Not that I know their names – she always gives them film-stars' nicknames – Stewart Granger, James Mason, Leslie Howard and so forth – I suppose she thinks it makes them more glamorous.

Friday. God, how I hate pigs! One of them sent me flying this morning – it knocked the bucket of swill out of my hand and pushed me over into the mud! Normally I avoid the creatures like the plague but May wasn't well – some sort of stomach upset – so I had to feed the brutes. That bloody Wop Dino had the nerve to laugh – I'll have to have a word with him. He'll be laughing on the other side of his face before too long.

Wednesday. There seems to be something the matter

with May – she looks terrible. At first I thought it was still the effects of her stomach upset, but it's more than that. She's been going around looking like death – dreadfully pale, she hasn't bothered to put any make-up on for the last few days and her hair's a mess. She's sullen and doesn't speak to anyone much and yesterday when her mother asked her if anything was the matter she was really rude, which isn't like her, she's normally a cheerful girl.

Sunday. To my surprise May got herself all done up and went off to the dance at the airfield as usual and I must say she's much more her old self today – at this moment I can hardly hear myself think for the loud dance music she's got on the wireless. I suppose it was just some sort of quarrel with her boyfriend – the one she calls Stewart Granger.

Wednesday. That Italian had the nerve to be insolent to me this morning. He refused to sluice down the yard – said it wasn't his job. I told him he'd better mind his manners or else I'd have to tell Mr Brown about his black-market activities. At first he pretended that he couldn't understand what I was saying, which is nonsense – his English is perfectly good. Then he blustered for a bit and then, when he saw I wasn't impressed, he started to whine and begged me not to say anything. I said I'd have to think about it and went away. That'll give *him* something to think about! Actually, I want to find out a lot more about all this before I say anything to anyone.

Sunday. May came back from the dance very late last night and today she's been in a strange mood – half broody, half excited. I think there's something she wants to tell me but she can't quite bring herself to do so.

Monday. Nearly a nasty accident today. I was ploughing the top field. It's a bit hilly, but I was managing quite well. Mr B. was doubtful at first about letting me use the tractor, but I told him I'd done the course at Wye College and since then I've used it quite a bit. This, of course, doesn't please our Italian friend, who was hoping to do the ploughing himself and is now carting stone up to Lower Barton field to mend the walls! Anyway, I was about half-way through, when the tractor turned over. Fortunately I was thrown clear. If it had fallen on top of me I would have been killed. As it was I've got some nasty bruises and I was covered in mud. At first Mr B. went on about women not being able to manage machinery, but later he discovered that the wheel had come loose and the extra pressure put on it going downhill had tipped it over. I am beginning to wonder, though, if it *was* an accident. I saw Dino in the yard this morning before I took the tractor out. I wouldn't put it past him to have loosened the wheel nuts.

Tuesday. I'm sure I was right about Dino and the tractor. This morning when Mr B. told him about the accident he gave me a very sly look and said very pointedly that Miss (he always calls me Miss in a rather slimy way) had better take care – or who knows what will happen! I don't know if he wanted me to be so badly injured that I'd be taken away or if he was just warning me. I shall have to think what to do.

Thursday. Of all the ridiculous things. I've got to take part in a Wings for Victory parade in Oxford. They've got people from the services and the NFS and Home Guard and so forth. Our District Organiser's just been round to say that they want a few Land Army girls 'to make a representative showing'. God knows where my hat is. I seem to remember throwing it on to the top of the wardrobe soon after I got here and I haven't seen it since. Mr B. is grumbling about my not being here

115

for the milking but I'm hardly doing it for *pleasure* as I pointed out to him. He's particularly annoyed because May has decided that she wants to come into Oxford to watch the parade – not particularly marvellous entertainment I would have thought, but I suppose anything is better than being stuck here – and he'll be short handed because it's not Dino's day for being here.

Monday. An absolutely vile day for the parade. Freezingly cold with an iron grey sky and a biting wind. We all assembled and were marched to the Cornmarket where the Mayor and various Council high-ups were standing on a platform. Then a Wing-Commander (rather good looking) made a speech about the value to the war effort of National Savings, which no one could hear properly because the microphone wasn't working very well. A couple of ATs collapsed in the bitter cold and the Red Cross contingent had to break ranks and attend to them. My fellow land girls were very scornful and said the — ATs ought to try pulling swedes in a frozen field if they wanted to know what — cold was really like! After it was over and we were all dispersing I happened to see the Council people getting down off the platform and to my amazement I saw Dino going up to one of them and saying something. The man looked a bit nervous and took him by the arm and led him behind one of the hoardings covered with National Savings posters. I couldn't stay to see how long they stayed talking because the other girls dragged me off to see if there was any beer at the Queen's Head. But I would dearly like to know what's going on there! As we were all going down the High I saw May and her airman – so that's why she wanted to go and watch. He's got dark wavy hair and is rather good looking in a flashy sort of way (I can see what she means about Stewart Granger).

He looked rather embarrassed at the way she was clinging to his arm.

Tuesday. I told May that I'd seen her with her young man. We were washing all the milking equipment in the dairy – a miserable job – my hands felt raw with the cold water. She went to the door and looked outside to see that no one was around. Then she stood for a moment looking down at the dirty water in the old stone sink and said slowly, 'Gwen, I'm in trouble.' I asked what sort of trouble and she said impatiently, 'In *trouble* – you know . . . ' 'Oh,' I said, 'you mean you're pregnant.' She seemed to find the word embarrassing and flushed. 'Yes,' she said. 'And I daren't tell my Dad – he'd kill me.' I thought she was exaggerating, dramatising the situation, because, as I've said, her parents dote on her. But she seemed really frightened. 'Have you told your mother?' I asked. 'No. She'd only tell him.' She seemed to be screwing herself up to ask me something and then blurted out, 'Gwen – do you know anyone?' 'Know anyone?' I echoed. 'Someone who could *do* something . . . ' 'An abortion?' 'Yes,' she whispered. 'No, sorry – not my line at all. What about the young man? Did he suggest that?' 'Yes.' She looked so wretched I couldn't help feeling sorry for her, though she had really no one to blame but herself for being such a little fool. 'You'll just have to make him face up to his responsibilities. Is he married?' 'Johnny? – that's his name – no he isn't, but his family's ever so well off – they wouldn't want him to marry someone like me.' 'He should have thought of that before he started messing around with you.' 'He's worried about something else. I oughtn't to be telling you about this – but, well, he and his friend (the one I call James Mason) have been doing something on the black market – just for a lark, really, I don't think they need the money, they

117

always seem to have plenty. Anyway, last week they stole a whole tanker full of petrol – aviation fuel they call it – it was ever so exciting, just like a film. They drove it off the airfield and along that track behind Hanger Wood – I told them about that, they were ever so pleased, they wouldn't have known about it else – and got round to the village that way and put it in Ray Burton's tank at the garage. They've got something else planned, but I don't know what it is – something really big.' 'You'll have to tell him that he's got to marry you and if he makes any difficulties you must say that you'll tell his Commanding Officer about all this black-market stuff – that'll bring him to heel.' 'Gwen, I couldn't!' 'Well, it's that or face your father.' I don't know if I've persuaded her, but I don't see why the man should get away with it . . .

There, maddeningly, the diary ended. The remaining pages were filled with accounts – details of her pay, tax and so forth. I wished to goodness that Molly had found the other notebook; it was infuriating not to know the end of the story.

What I had read only confirmed my opinion of Gwen Richmond. Even as a young woman she had obviously been totally self-centred and eager to manipulate other people's lives. I wondered what had happened to the wretched May and if Dino had got away with all his nefarious activities. One day I would find out from Molly where the farm was and go and have a look at it – rather like going to look at a place that had been the setting of a novel.

Chapter Eleven

'I've told the parents about Pamela,' Tony said next morning as he and I were making toast in the kitchen. 'Mother's invited them to Sunday lunch tomorrow.'

When he'd gone Betty and I had a little chat about it over our second cups of coffee.

'What's she like?' Betty asked. 'I gather you've met her.'

'Only because Tony wanted me to tell her what a terrific success Peter, Mother and I living together was,' I explained hastily, though Betty wasn't at all the sort of mother who resents her children confiding in other people. 'She's a nice girl – very shy – what you might call "biddable". She's devoted to her mother and they both *dote* on Tony!'

'Good gracious! Well I'm absolutely delighted that he's found someone – he never seemed at all interested. Harriet brought several really *splendid* girls back from Greenham Common, but he simply ignored them.'

'Well, he found Pamela all for himself,' I said.

'Tony says that she's leaving the Bodleian.'

'Yes, she's going to do some work for the University Press. But, quite frankly, I don't think she's a career girl.'

Betty's face fell and I smiled.

'I think Tony has found himself what used to be described as a home-maker.'

'Oh well, it's early days yet,' Betty said. 'Just look at me!'

* * *

We were a large party that Sunday lunchtime because Betty insisted that Michael and I should be included.

'It will be much easier for them if it's not just family and they've met you already and feel comfortable with you!'

Any doubts I might have had about how the Turners would fit in were swiftly dispelled. Robert was marvellous with Mrs Turner, discussing her treatment with his usual enthusiasm – obviously only his sense of professional etiquette stopped him from launching into a vigorous condemnation of her present GP and I felt that it was only a matter of time before he would have her whisked into the Nuffield Orthopedic and generally sorted out. Betty, too, was delighted to have what was practically a captive audience – and one, moreover, who seemed genuinely interested in her various projects. I foresaw many droppings-in on Mrs Turner to discuss the latest strategy in some new campaign.

I began to wonder, indeed, if the Turners were not in danger of being totally taken over and didn't dare to catch Michael's eye when Betty asked Pamela if she would like to go with her to a meeting about nuclear waste.

'We're going to mark out the way they take the lorries by putting up placards saying "nuclear waste route" all round the ring road.'

Still, I was sure that the newly confident Tony was quite capable of keeping his parents within bounds.

When it was obvious that they were all getting on splendidly and didn't need any outside help, I said I would drive Michael back to Oxford.

Because it was a lovely sunny Sunday the roads were crowded and there was a solid jam of traffic just past the Blenheim roundabout. Michael wound down the window and peered out.

'It seems to be a crack of doom situation,' he said regarding the long line of cars stretching into the distance.

120

We sat peacefully in the warm sunlight. The sky was a brilliant blue and on either side of the dual carriageway there was a glorious white froth of cow parsley. For a while we neither of us spoke, then Michael said tentatively, 'I've come to a sort of decision, if that's not too grand a word for it. I think I'd like to go to the College of Law and be a solicitor like Pa.'

I smiled encouragingly, but didn't say anything and he went on, speaking very rapidly.

'I think there's still time to register for September – I've got to have my degree of course, so fingers crossed and all that – I don't know if we can afford it – the course costs quite a bit and living in London is frightfully expensive, and it's for two years – but I thought I *might* be a lodger with Cousin Hilary, she's always been marvellous about my staying there in the Long Vac – anyway, I could find out what it would all cost . . . '

His voice trailed away and he looked at me enquiringly.

I tried to blink away the tears that I knew would embarrass him and said, 'Pa would have been so pleased. What made you decide?'

'I've been thinking about it for ages and then I talked to William – you remember William, my year, reading Law – and it all sounded pretty interesting . . . '

I approved of William, a solid young man, over six foot with a shock of bright red hair and an imperturbable manner. I always felt, somehow, that Michael would be *safe* in his company. I now felt a glow of gratitude towards him as well.

'Of course we'll afford it somehow and Cousin Hilary is a brilliant idea. 'She'll love having you there – you'll be able to feed the cats for her when she goes away.'

A loud hooting made me aware that the traffic was now moving and we completed the journey into Oxford happily making plans for Michael's future.

I managed to nip into a parking space in Museum Street and walked along with him to his college. The gardens were looking marvellous and we strolled round the corner of the chapel and sat down on a seat from which we could contemplate the rather surrealist statue of an eccentric former dean. The bronze torso merging into the bronze chair usually irritated me, but today, overhung by spring foliage and surrounded by a carpet of bluebells it seemed an agreeable piece of whimsy.

Michael was talking about Tony and Pamela and the Bodleian.

'*Not* the place I would go to choose a bride – they all frighten me to death!'

'Well if you will go in there wearing full biking gear, complete with boots and helmet you must admit they have every reason for looking at you sideways! Anyway, Pamela is a sweet girl.'

'A bread-and-butter miss,' he said, 'but just right for old Tony, who will now become a Victorian paterfamilias with a watch-chain across his waistcoat and eleven children.'

Talk of the Bodleian brought me back with a jolt to the mystery of Gwen Richmond and I now gave Michael a brief summary of what had happened and what I suspected.

'Poor old Tony, what a vile thing to have happened. She sounds a real platinum-plated bitch, if you ask me, and simply asked to be batted over the head.'

'That's as maybe, but as a future upholder of the law you must admit that people can't be allowed to go around batting people over the head, however unspeakable they may be.'

'You've got a fair old number of suspects. There's those two old Arthurian birds and Gwen whatsit's sister, and Pamela, of course.'

'No, not Pamela,' I said quickly.

'Suit yourself, but she ought to be on the list, and Tony, too, come to think of it.'

'Now you're being ridiculous.'

'Well, I agree they're neither of them likely, but in a detective story they'd be the strongest suspects.'

'We are *not*,' I informed him severely, 'living in a detective story and Tony is my godson.'

'Right. No godson shall be deemed to be a murderer – I wonder if Crippen had a godmother?'

I disregarded this flippancy and said, 'I'm a bit suspicious, too, of this Dr Lassiter. She was there in the Bodleian on the day in question and I have a feeling that she used to be in Athens when Gwen was. Actually, I'd like to have a chat with her. I wonder . . . do you have the Hoard with you here in Oxford?'

The Hoard, I must explain, was a collection of ancient coins that Peter had bought in the Middle East when he was out there in the Army at the end of the war. We always used to joke that they were worth a fortune and were our little nest egg for a rainy day. When Michael was sixteen Peter handed them over to him with stern admonitions to keep them safe for a Real Emergency.

'Yes, I have. I was going to show them to Hardwick, he's quite a collector, but I haven't got round to it yet.'

'Could I borrow them for a few days? Dr Lassiter is in the coin room at the Ashmolean and I could use them as an excuse for getting to see her.'

'I don't quite see how you propose to make the leap from old coins to murder. "How interesting about the tetradrachms and by the way did you murder Gwen Richmond?"'

'I expect I'll think of something,' I said vaguely. 'Anyway people do tend to tell me things – it's all those years of practice with listening to the Meals on Wheels people.'

'*Not* quite the same thing – but if anyone can get anything out of her, you can!'

We went back through the quadrangle to Michael's room. As always, I tried to shut my eyes to the wild disorder but had to be restrained by Michael from picking up books and scattered essay papers from the floor.

'*No*, Ma! Incredible though it may seem to you there is a sort of sublime order about this seeming chaos, rather like the organisation of the spheres. Remove but one sheet of paper and the whole structure falls apart. Meanwhile I will make you a cup of tea and get you the Hoard.'

He plugged a kettle in, saying, 'The whole electrical system here is pre-Faraday but it seems to work', and unearthed two mugs from beneath a pile of *Proceedings of the Society for Mediaeval Studies*. I tried not to notice if the mugs had been washed or not and watched him make the tea.

'Oh good, a new packet of chocolate digestives,' he said, tearing off the wrapping and casting it on to the floor.

I picked it up, biting back the reproof that rose to my lips. I've got this compulsive need to pick up bits of paper – the sight of litter makes me really quite ill! Michael stopped pouring the tea for a moment and said, 'Oh, Ma, *really!*' as he always does on such occasions.

He gave me the mug and a biscuit and, opening a tin marked 'TEA', tumbled out a pile of old silver coins.

As I held them in my hand I felt, as I always do, an almost superstitious awe when I think that these objects have been in existence since before the birth of Christ.

'They're really in remarkably good nick,' Michael said, picking one up and examining it lovingly. ' "Extremely fine", is that what they call it?'

'I think so. I'll take great care of them, of course, and give them back to you as soon as I've been able to see the Lassiter woman.'

I found a plastic bag in my handbag and stowed them carefully away. That evening, when all the aspects of the visit by Pamela and her mother had been fully gone into, I managed to take Tony to one side and ask him if he'd managed to make a list of the people who had been in

Room 45 on the afternoon that Gwen Richmond was killed.

'Well – yes, in a way, but it's not much help, there weren't many people in – it was a Friday afternoon, you see. Well, apart from Dr Lassiter there were only two rather nice American academics – a Dr Hjelmaa from Stanford University and a Dr Fergus from Lehigh. And I honestly don't think that either of *them* will do as a suspect, because they were only in on that one day and they haven't been back since, and neither of them so much as *mentioned* Gwen.'

'And that was all?'

'Oh yes, there *was* Professor Mainwaring, but he's ninety if he's a day and almost completely gaga!'

'So we're left with Freda Lassiter. Was she there the whole afternoon?'

'Well, she was certainly there when we had to clear everyone out, after I'd found . . . '

'But was she there *all* afternoon or did she pop out for a bit?'

'Oh dear, I think she might have gone out for a short while – I'm afraid I didn't notice – people do, you know, to the loo or out for a cup of tea . . . '

'But she would have known her way about the place? She could have found Gwen's room?'

'I expect so. She was in and out quite a bit.'

'Did Gwen ever say anything about her?'

'Well, yes, as a matter of fact. She talked about her in a sort of sneering way, if you know what I mean. She often did that with people she didn't get on well with. I gathered that she *had* known Freda Lassiter when they were both at the British School in Athens, but she, Dr Lassiter, that is, left – in a bit of a hurry and under a cloud if Gwen's hints were anything to go by – a couple of years before Gwen did.'

'What do you think of Dr Lassiter?'

'She's very woolly and scatterbrained, rather neurotic

I should think, looks as if she's living on the edge of her nerves. I honestly can't see her planning a murder.'

'But don't you see – it needn't have been planned. Say Gwen was blackmailing her, in her own particularly horrible way, and simply pushed her too far – over the edge, in fact. So Dr Lassiter bats her over the head,' I found I was using Michael's phrase and amended it, 'I mean, she snatches up that large book, Horsley's whatever it is, and hits Gwen over the head. *Then* she realises what she's done and tries to cover it up by dislodging the bookcases. She's quite a hefty woman, she could have done it perfectly easily.'

I found I was building up the case against Dr Lassiter with some enthusiasm, because, my conscience said, she was someone I didn't really know and so it didn't seem so bad to regard her as a prime suspect.

Tony looked doubtful.

'I suppose it's possible – I suppose I just can't think of a woman being a murderer.'

'That's your nice nature,' I said, smiling. 'Anyway, I'll see what I can find out. Meanwhile, can you do something for me? Do you know anyone in the Duke Humfrey who might be able to confirm that Arthur Fitzgerald was working there on the day in question? I'm sure he's a well-known figure. It would help if we could establish alibis – or not, as the case may be, for the major suspects.'

Tony had been very reluctant to think of Fitz or Elaine as suspects, although he admitted that they had a very strong motive for killing Gwen. He had also rejected Molly Richmond as a suspect on the grounds that she was a friend of his mother! Tony is a sweet boy but there are times when I feel that I could shake him.

'Oh yes, I'll ask Dick Fisher – he may well have been on duty then.'

Cleopatra, who had been sitting on the draining board lashing her tail from side to side to the imminent danger of

126

the crockery left there to drain, decided that she had been ignored long enough and gave a loud cry. Tony turned the tap on for her and she batted at the water several times with a delicate fawn paw and then jumped into the sink and began to lap noisily at the water as it ran down the plug-hole.

'And she's got a perfectly good bowl of water too,' said Tony ruefully.

'I know! Foss is just the same – he much prefers drinking from some awful stagnant puddle in the garden!'

Tony turned the tap off, slung Cleopatra across his shoulders and went into the hall. As they went up the stairs he said, 'Gwen once said that Freda Lassiter was a fool about men, but she didn't go into any details so I don't know what she meant.'

'Oh well,' I said, 'I may be able to enlighten you tomorrow.'

The word 'cosy' isn't the first adjective that springs to mind in connection with the Ashmolean, but because I always think of it as 'my' museum – one that I am very familiar with and where I feel at home – that is how I regard it. I know my way around there (give or take a rearrangement or an exhibition or two) and there are many old friends among the exhibits that I try to pop in to see when I'm in Oxford. There's a mummified cat in the Egyptian section in the basement that reminds me irresistibly of Cleopatra, a couple of seventeenth-century paintings upstairs and a statue of a Roman matron who is the image of my friend Pauline. As I passed through the classical section I paused to greet her, marvelling as I always did at the splendidly intricate styling of her hair.

I hadn't telephoned for an appointment with Freda Lassiter because I had the feeling that valuing coins wasn't actually part of her job, but I hoped to take her by surprise – in several ways. An amiable young man in the Heberden Room said he thought she was in her office and would I like to follow him and I blessed my good fortune. He ushered me into a tiny office, hardly more than a glass cubby-hole, and I found myself face to face with her and suddenly rather nervous. As I always do when I'm nervous, I plunged in straight away, talking rather fast so that she really didn't have time to query my being there.

'*Do* forgive me barging in like this without an appointment or anything, but I was just passing, well, not just *passing* exactly, but in Oxford for a short time so I thought . . . well this mutual friend said you would be the person to ask about these *coins*. I'm afraid you'll think it's an awful cheek, but I've been meaning to do something about them for *ages* – well you know how it is – and if they *are* valuable then I ought to keep them in the bank or something – though that does always seem a shame – to keep things locked away when they could be giving so much pleasure, don't you agree?'

Looking slightly dazed (as well she might) she seized on the one word that seemed to make some sort of sense to her.

'Do you have some coins you want identifying? Do, please, sit down.'

'If you would be so kind.' I began to burrow in my handbag. 'I really haven't the faintest idea about them. My husband brought them back from the Middle East after the war.' I fished out the plastic bag and handed it to her and she took the coins out carefully and laid them on her desk.

On her own ground she seemed much calmer and better organised than when I had seen her before, though I noticed as she spread the coins out in front of her that her nails were bitten right down to the quick.

She examined the silver coins intently and for some time.

'What you appear to have here are some very remarkable coins. These are Antiochid tetradrachms, Syrian,

128

first century BC; these are cistophori of Augustus; these are denarii of the Emperor Otho; and this is a silver tetradrachm of Antony and Cleopatra – very rare indeed.'

For a moment all thought of Gwen Richmond's murder and my real reason for being there vanished from my mind and I reached out and picked up one of the coins, holding it in my hand, feeling it almost as a living presence.

'Good gracious,' I said inadequately. 'Are they valuable then?'

Dr Lassiter looked at me sadly.

'I'm sorry,' she said. 'I'm afraid I have misled you. I said *appear* to have. I very much regret – but – well they're forgeries.'

'Forgeries?'

'Yes. With coins as rare as these there was at one time quite a market in forgeries – they were made in Beirut which was the centre for forgery and distribution at that time. I'm very sorry. Of course, you mustn't just take my word for it. I will give you the name of a colleague at the British Museum who will give you a second opinion . . . '

She scribbled a name on a piece of paper and handed it to me. Then, making conversation to give me time to recover myself she said, 'Did you say we had a mutual friend?'

With a great wrench I pulled myself together – I would think of Peter and Michael later – and tried to find a form of words that would get the result I wanted.

'Yes, indeed. Gwen Richmond – well I know her sister better really – but she,' I left the personal pronoun deliberately vague, 'told me *all* about you.'

Dr Lassiter's calm authoritative manner slid away from her and an agitated note came into her voice.

'All about me?'

'About being together in Athens. Though, of course, you left . . . '

'She told you about that?'

129

The voice was raised now and anxious. I was right about her being neurotic, I thought.

'Yes,' I lied, feeling rather mean.

'She told you what a fool I made of myself.'

'She didn't put it quite like that,' I said.

'Oh, she wouldn't – I expect she told you that I did something criminal – yes, well, stealing an artefact from a dig *is* criminal. It is also the most unethical thing an archaeologist can do.'

Her face was flushed and she spoke in a harsh sort of whisper. I began to feel nervous at the response I had evoked – it was as if Gwen Richmond's name was a sort of trigger which had set her off. I had the feeling that she was talking about all this because, in some way, she had to and that my presence was almost irrelevant. I tried to speak soothingly.

'But surely many eminent archaeologists from Schliemann on . . . '

She broke in impatiently.

'It is betraying a trust. It is unforgivable.'

'Then why did you . . . ?'

'For a man, of course. Women are such fools . . . '

'I see.'

These simple words seemed to calm her and she spoke almost ruefully.

'He was Greek and much older than I was, very rich and important. He had this magnificent flat in Kolonaki – full of the most beautiful things. He was a notable collector. There was so little I could give him and I was desperate to keep his interest. It was easy for me to steal it – but they found out. I had to beg for it back – you can imagine the humiliation. No one wanted to make a fuss, relations between the British School and the Government would have suffered. They simply sent me away.'

'I'm so sorry,' I said, and indeed, it would have been difficult not to pity her and her misery in remembering.

'I didn't think anyone knew except the Director and

Professor Meredith, who was in charge of the dig, but Gwen found out somehow – probably listened at a door, that's the sort of person she is – was.' She looked at me sharply. 'I'm surprised that she told you about it – she usually liked to keep these secrets to herself – it gave her a feeling of power.'

'She didn't tell me outright,' I said, feeling more and more uncomfortable. 'She sort of hinted and left me to piece things together . . . ' My voice trailed away.

'I don't imagine that I'm the only one she knew secrets about,' Dr Lassiter went on. 'I expect quite a lot of people are glad that she is dead. I'm sorry if she was a friend of yours. But you must have known what sort of person she was.'

'As I said, I know her sister Molly much better.'

'In fact,' Freda Lassiter went on, 'I wouldn't be at all surprised if someone killed her.'

I took a chance and said, 'I quite agree with you. I'm almost sure she *was* murdered.'

She looked at me enquiringly and then gave a short laugh.

'And you think I murdered her? Is *that* why you came to see me?'

'No, of course not,' I said hastily, 'at least – I *did* want to know about the coins – but I must confess I was curious to see you . . . '

'I *was* in the building when she was killed,' she said, 'and I *did* leave Room 45 for half an hour. Actually I went to Blackwell's to buy a book – I suppose the man at the desk might remember me going in and out.' She looked at me quizzically. 'That is, if you think I need an alibi.'

I had no doubt George's memory would be pretty reliable on this point. If I were to ask him. There was an embarrassed pause and then she spoke, suddenly, breaking the silence.

'*Do* you think I killed her?'

131

I looked at her for a moment and said, 'No. I don't believe you did.'

She gave a little laugh. 'Why? Don't you think I'm capable of it?'

'No. I don't.'

'I had a motive, of sorts. I hated her, really *hated* . . . and then I obviously wouldn't want anyone here to know why I left Athens. They were very good there – they gave me references . . . '

'No, you couldn't kill anyone, no matter how strong a motive you had.'

'What makes you so sure of that,' she asked curiously.

'Because you're too like me – I would have done what you did in similar circumstances. I would have hated, as you did. But I couldn't take a human life and I don't believe you could either.'

'You're right, of course. I couldn't have killed her. But I'm very glad someone else did!'

I thought of Pamela saying the same thing. How terrible it was to have made people so wretched that even perfectly nice people rejoice at your death.

'Are you trying to find out who did kill her?' Freda Lassiter asked.

'If I can.'

'Why? Who are you – some sort of detective?'

'Goodness, no! I suppose it's because I hate any sort of mystery – a dreadful kind of curiosity. And besides, my godson, Tony Stirling, who works in the Bodleian, found the body. He was very upset about it and I want to lay a ghost for him if I can.'

'Well, I wish you luck – in a way.'

'Thank you.'

She looked down and saw the coins on the table.

'I'm sorry about your coins. I do hope you weren't banking on their being valuable.'

'No. It was mostly sentiment, really. My husband,

132

who bought them, died a couple of years ago – I just wanted them to be something special for his sake.'

With a quick movement I shovelled the coins into their plastic bag. Now there was no mystery, no magic. They were just flat discs of metal.

'I'm sorry,' she repeated.

'Thank you,' I said, and held out my hand. She shook it and we smiled at each other.

'Goodbye,' I said, 'and thank you.'

I made my way back into the classical section of the museum, feeling upset and disorientated and sat down on a leather bench near my Roman matron. I felt a pang, almost a physical pain of disappointment about the coins and hoped that Michael would not be similarly distressed. I also wanted to come to grips with my reaction to Freda Lassiter's story. For some reason it had moved me deeply, perhaps because in her I saw what I might have become if I hadn't had the sturdy rock of a good marriage to rest upon. There but for the grace of God . . . I felt churned up and unhappy. But gradually the cool stone figures around me, carefully delineated representations of men and women, influential or unknown, but now all long dead, soothed and restored me. I was staring in a peaceful non-thinking way at a crumbling marble statue of a couchant lion when a voice beside me said, 'Are you thinking deep Shakespearean thoughts?'

I looked up and saw Bill Howard regarding me with some amusement.

'I'm sorry?'

He gestured towards the statue.

'"Devouring Time that blunts the lion's paws,"' he said. 'I thought you might be contemplating immortality.'

'No,' I replied, 'just brooding.'

'Now that is something that can be done much better in the Randolph over a delicious tea. Won't you join me?

Today's the day for my weekly shot of culture and I'm longing for an excuse to have a little break.'

Feeling considerably cheered I got up from the bench, smiled approvingly at the lion and followed Bill out of the Ashmolean, across the road and into the comforting warmth and solidity of the Randolph.

Chapter Twelve

I am an absolute sucker for atmosphere. Put me in a splendid, old-fashioned hotel with panelled walls and rich dark furnishings, add all the delightful panoply of an English teatime, with a piano somewhere in the distance playing Gershwin, then I positively beam with pleasure.

'This *is* nice,' I said. '*Just* what I needed.'

'You certainly looked pretty down when I came across you in the museum over there. Is anything the matter?'

He looked at me with some concern and I experienced once again that little tug of attraction I had felt when we first met, then I relaxed and realised that I could treat him as a friend to chat to, to confide in even. I suddenly felt the need to talk to someone who would understand.

'I've had a peculiar afternoon,' I said.

I told him about the coins and he seemed to know immediately how I felt.

'As if you've lost something precious,' he said. 'Not the money – I can see that – but something you and your husband and son had together. I'm so sorry.'

'The coins were only part of it,' I said, and told him about Gwen Richmond's murder and some of my investigations so far. Not all of them, of course. I couldn't betray Pamela and I didn't like to mention Fitz and Elaine for obvious reasons. I concentrated on Dr Lassiter and Molly Richmond. He listened attentively and asked the occasional question. When I had finished I was aware that it all sounded rather thin and I hoped he wouldn't

135

think that I was just a foolish busybody.

He stirred his tea thoughtfully and said slowly, 'You're really sure she was murdered – it couldn't have been just an accident?'

'I don't *think* so. Tony was very positive about the glasses and about where that book would have been.'

'Yes, I see. Well now. Isn't this exciting, we have a murder on our hands.' He passed me a plate of small, intricately wrought cakes. 'Do have one of these, they look so good. I love mysteries. I always promised myself that when I retired I would spend my time cooking and reading mystery stories. It hasn't happened yet, but this is even better. What can I do to help?'

'I don't think you can actually *do* anything at the moment. Mind you, there may come a time when I may ask you to put on a false beard and *lurk* somewhere. Seriously, though, until Tony's made some enquiries for me and checked a few times – it's so handy that he's in the Bodleian and can ask people things – so that we can see who was where on "the Day", well, there's not much to be done.'

'You must keep me posted, though, and give me progress reports. And I absolutely insist on being there for the final dénouement, when you gather everyone together in the panelled library and tell us how it was done!'

'That's a promise.'

I glanced at my watch. 'Goodness, I must be going. I've enjoyed myself so much the time has simply *gone*. I promised Michael I'd drop in on him on my way back to Woodstock. Thank you so much for the tea – and the sympathy.'

'It was great seeing you. Look – why don't you and your son have dinner with me one evening this week. I'd so much like to meet him. I'll give you my phone number, then you can call and let me know which day is best for you.'

He fished in his jacket pocket for a pen and pulled out a whole collection of objects on to the table – bits of paper, a crumpled programme, a couple of chocolate wrappers, a nail-file, a comb, an assortment of small coins, two ballpoint pens, several pencils and a leaflet about a carpet sale in a church hall in the Cowley Road.

He smiled ruefully. 'Now you know my guilty secret – I'm incapable of throwing anything away.'

'Compared with my dear son that is as nothing.'

He straightened out the programme, which was a National Theatre cast list for *The Seagull*, and, selecting one of the pens, wrote a phone number in the margin.

'There you are – everything comes in useful sometime! Here's my number. I'm staying in a house in Jericho that belongs to a friend who's in Germany for a while – it's really cute, like a doll house. You must come and see it.'

He began gathering up the scattered objects on the table.

'Now you *don't* need these,' I said firmly, picking out the chocolate wrappers, 'or, I imagine *this*?' I held up the leaflet.

'People are always pushing things into your hands in Oxford. Either that or confronting you with clipboards and asking damfool questions about your TV viewing habits. You are right. As a great concession you may throw those away.'

'I will take them away and put them tidily in some waste bin,' I said. 'It will be a great treat for me because Michael won't let me throw away as much as a bent paper clip or a piece of wrapping paper.'

We smiled at each other and I felt how cosy and nice he was to be with. As we went out into the lobby of the Randolph a notice on a stand caught my eye.

'Oh, do look,' I said.

The notice read:

Dorothy Sayers Society
27th May. Luncheon (£13 excluding wine)
Peter Wimsey Centenary
Speaker: The Dean of Balliol:
'Oxford and the Balliol of Wimsey's time'

'Oh *wouldn't* you like to go to that!' I exclaimed.
'But I suppose you have to be a member.'

'We could gate-crash. I'm glad you're a Sayers fan
too. To my mind she's the greatest.'

We walked along the Broad animatedly arguing the
merits of our favourite novels.

'The Harriet ones *best* of course, but then of the
others, if you could only have one which would it be?'

'Oh, *Nine Tailors* -- no question about it.'

'Ye-es, I don't know, though. I think *Murder Must
Advertise* for me – although . . . '

We stood on the corner of Catte Street.

'I must go back into the Bodleian,' Bill said.

'And I must go and find Michael.'

'Do you realise that it was almost exactly fifty-five
years ago, and almost on this very spot, that Peter and
Harriet got engaged.'

'There should be a plaque,' I said. 'In Latin.'

'Absolutely. Let me see – "*Hic Peter Wimsey et Harriet
Vane sese despondierunt 27 May 1935*".'

'Aren't you brilliant! How do you know the date
so exactly?'

'The letters at the beginning of *Busman's Honeymoon*.'

'Of *course* – stupid of me. I'll ring you.'

'Make it soon! Goodbye.'

I crossed the road and went towards Michael's college
feeling almost light-hearted, something that would have
seemed impossible just over an hour ago.

Michael was in his room deep in the throes of an
essay, which to judge by the opened books scattered
about was on some aspect of the English Civil War.

'Causes of or events arising from?' I asked. 'Or aren't questions at your level as simple as that?'

'Constitutional junk,' he said. 'It doesn't matter much what the question is as long as you get the word dysfunction into your answer somehow. Any luck with the Hoard?'

'Oh, love, I'm so sorry, but I'm afraid it's bad news. They're forgeries.'

I told him what Dr Lassiter had said and took the coins out of my bag.

He picked up one of them and weighed it in his hand. 'Oh well,' he said, 'there goes my inheritance.'

'What are you going to do with them,' I asked.

'Keep them of course. Pa gave them to me, after all – I wouldn't want to get rid of them. I'm glad he didn't know.'

'Yes. Bless you – you're so much more sensible than I am.'

'Yes, Ma. I keep telling you so. So – what about the Lassiter as murderer?'

For the second time that day I described my talk with Freda Lassiter.

'I'm positive she didn't do it.'

'Woman's intuition, eh?'

'Something like that.'

'Oh well, back to the drawing board.'

'Yes. I mustn't keep you from your work, but I wondered if you felt you could spare the time to take an evening off – Bill Howard's asked us to have dinner with him. Though I'm sure he would understand if you're too busy with revision.'

'The prospect of a decent meal is very appealing. I need building up at this time, as I'm sure you'll agree.'

'OK. Any day this week. When?'

'Wednesday or Thursday. I shall be delighted to inspect your new beau.'

'No beau of mine. Of Fitz, I think.'

'Ah, I see. Pity. I thought I might have got you off my hands. Can I, then, inspect him as a suspect? If he's working in Room 45 I'm sure we could find *some* sort of motive for him.'

'Sorry, you can't even have him as a suspect. Not only does he have no conceivable motive but he wasn't even there at the time – he was in London. He went up for the day with a friend.'

'Oh well, I shall concentrate on the free-meal aspect. I hope he takes us somewhere expensive, though try to warn him off *nouvelle cuisine*. Remember the time when Uncle Jack took us to that chi-chi place in Covent Garden and I was so starving I had to get a Big Mac on the way home.'

'I'll phone him then and give him a choice of dates.'

I checked in my bag to make sure that I had the telephone number and glancing at the programme that he had written it on I exclaimed, 'Oh well, he's even got a proper alibi. This performance was on the day that Gwen Richmond was murdered.'

'Quel disappointment.'

I picked up my bag and prepared to go.

'Have you got something respectable to wear?'

'I shall wear my best biking jacket with the Yamaha badge – of *course* I've got something respectable!'

'Well, make sure you wear a tie.'

'*Yes*, Ma.'

'All right, I'm off. Work hard. God bless.'

When Tony came home in the evening I followed him into the kitchen when he went to feed Cleopatra and told him about Freda Lassiter.

'A dead end, I'm afraid.'

'And your friend Fitz is another, I fear. He was certainly in Duke Humfrey that afternoon. Dick Fisher knows him well. Apparently he's something of a thorn in the flesh of the people there – always complaining about something. That Friday he made quite a fuss because a

140

certain edition of Browning wasn't available – it was with Conservation – he was quite unreasonable, Dick said.'

'Oh dear, another dead end. And no sign of Elaine, I suppose?'

'None whatsoever.'

'Door after door shut in our faces.'

Cleopatra, who had been daintily picking at her plate of cooked rabbit (best boned Chinese from Sainsbury's), stopped eating and began to scrape with her paw around her plate in a pointed way. Then she looked up at Tony, gave a loud wail and went to the kitchen door where she demanded peremptorily to be let out.

Betty came bustling in.

'Robert's actually in for supper this evening – go and chat to him while I finish off here.'

'Can't I do anything to help?'

'No, you go and talk to Robert else he'll go wandering off to the greenhouse and I'll never get him in again.'

Most unusually, Robert was actually sitting on the sofa reading the *Oxford Mail*. He looked up as I came in and said, 'Managed to get Mrs Drury's weight down to eleven stone, so she can have that hernia op. at last. They couldn't have done it before, it would've been like cutting into a hot-air balloon!'

I expressed pleasure at Mrs Drury's forthcoming surgery and asked – more to stem a flood of similar information, than because I particularly cared – if there was anything interesting in the paper.

'Not much – oh yes, the Council are giving that new development the go-ahead.'

'Where's that?'

'Near Folly Bridge – absolute scandal, shouldn't be allowed.'

He read aloud ' "Councillor Dino Torcello said that the new development would bring prosperity to a previously run-down area." ' He snorted. 'Prosperity to Councillor Torcello, he means. I suppose he wants to put

141

yet another restaurant in there, as well as the two he's got in the centre of town *and* the original one in Woodstock.'

Betty came into the room with the sherry and some glasses.

'Did you see this, Betty? That Torcello man's going to litter up the whole of the Folly Bridge area with his confounded trattorias!'

She handed me a glass and said, 'It really is too bad! I thought we'd reached rock bottom with the St Aldate's Centre, but now there's the Clarendon one – that hideous blue! – and if they're going to ruin Folly Bridge as well . . . '

'I never trusted that Torcello man.' He turned to me. 'His first wife was a patient of mine – pleasant woman. She was a war widow when she married Torcello – had a nice little restaurant in Woodstock. He was an Italian prisoner of war.'

'What!'

I sat bolt upright, all attention now.

'Yes. You wouldn't think she'd have married an *Italian* when her husband had just been killed in the war. I wasn't there then, of course, but I believe there was a lot of talk about it in Woodstock at the time.'

'I can imagine.'

'To be fair,' Betty said, 'her husband died at Dunkirk – nothing to do with the Italians.'

'Did he work at one of the farms near by,' I asked, hardly able to believe my luck.

'Somewhere near Kidlington, I believe. What was the name of that old chap who used to own it – Smith, Brown, something like that. Jack Proctor bought it when the old man gave up – paid a ridiculous price, it was badly run-down . . . Anyway,' he took a breath and continued with relish, 'it was obvious that Torcello only married the poor woman to get his hands on the restaurant.'

'Mind you,' Betty said, 'he did build it up into a splendid place.'

'They say that was all done on black-market stuff,' Robert said vigorously, 'things other people couldn't get.'

'Well, it's very nice now. We might go there one evening while Sheila is here.'

'That would be lovely. Did you say his first wife died?'

'Yes. Cancer of the oesophagus, poor soul. Then he married the girl who did the book-keeping, quite a young girl. His sons didn't like it but, of course, they were making a good thing out of running the Oxford restaurants so they couldn't say much.'

'Which are the Oxford ones,' I asked.

'There's the Murano in the High and the Scala in St Michael's Street. He's got this enormous house out beyond Finstock – one of Murray's patients I believe – must be worth a packet now. Got himself on the Council, you see, got it made – never looked back!'

Robert's views on local government were forthright to say the least.

'Oxford was destroyed by the Victorians, really,' he said, harking back to an earlier theme, 'when they pulled down the mediaeval bits and put up all those dreary little houses that people are paying a fortune for now. All the atmosphere went then. Look at Cambridge and how different *that* is.' Robert had been born in Cambridge and he and I batted the old Oxford/Cambridge argument back and forth for a bit while Betty went out to see to the supper.

'Yes, well, I'll give you the Backs, but our university is *older* than your technical college in East Anglia!' I ended up defiantly, as I usually did.

Tony, who had come in during our discussion, if such it could be called, laughed. 'I seem to remember hearing this conversation before.'

He was interrupted by an extremely loud wailing noise from upstairs. Robert who had gone back to the *Oxford Mail* said absently, 'That cat will have to go!'

Tony smiled affectionately at his father and went up

143

to investigate. He called to me, 'Do come and look Sheila!'

I went upstairs to find Cleopatra perched on top of a door, her eyes enormous with excitement, looking just like Tenniel's Cheshire Cat.

'Oh, clever girl!' I said fondly.

Cleopatra gave another cry.

'Yes, we can see you,' Tony said and she blinked at him lovingly.

'How does she get up there?'

'Well, actually, she climbs up my dressing gown on the back of the door, but we don't admit that because she likes us to think that she's leapt up there in one bound! She bellows like this partly for attention, but partly because she can't get down!'

He lifted her carefully off the top of the door and settled her on his shoulder.

'Come along you wicked girl and we'll find something nice for you.'

'Tony, just a minute before we go down. I've just found out something extraordinary. You remember Gwen Richmond's diary?'

'Yes, of course.'

'Well do you remember – one of the people on that farm she was planning to blackmail was that Italian prisoner of war?'

'Yes.'

'Well – you'll never guess! He's still in Oxford. He stayed on after the war – your father's just been telling me – and now he's a highly respectable man and a local councillor into the bargain!'

'Good heavens!'

'If Gwen Richmond came across him when she finally got back to Oxford – and, being a councillor his name would be constantly plastered all over the *Oxford Mail* and *Times* – then, knowing what we do about the sort of person she was, it seems a safe bet that she looked him

144

up – went to one of the restaurants perhaps, that would be easy – and started blackmailing him all over again.'

'Torcello,' Tony said slowly, 'the name does sound familiar.'

'Well he *is* a local councillor. You would have come across his name a lot of times – especially if your mother came up against him in one of her protests!'

'No, it's not that— '

'Anyway,' I broke in impatiently, 'he has a lot more to lose now than in the war, especially if his fortune was founded on shady dealings. He'd be particularly sensitive to criticism – as a councillor, that is. So he would need to keep her quiet.'

'Yes, but— '

'I know what you're going to say and that's the infuriating thing! He could have found out that she was working in the Bodleian, I suppose, but there's no way he could have got in to kill her without a reader's ticket. Oh well! It was a nice theory.'

Feeling very deflated I followed Tony down the stairs, Cleopatra smirking at me from his shoulder.

After supper when Robert disappeared to the garden and Tony went off to play badminton, Betty said, 'Shall we watch the box? There's not much on. Oh, I know – I recorded *Love Story* the other week in case we felt like a good weepy. It's *not* as good as the old ones, I know, but better than those depressing comedy programmes this evening.'

'There's nothing like a good piece of sentimentality for making one cry,' I remarked as we dabbed at our eyes at the end of the film. 'Proper tragedy doesn't do it, of course, because of catharsis, or whatever it is, but something really sentimental always has me in floods.'

'Mm,' Betty agreed. 'You're absolutely right. There is definitely a place for the second-rate in our lives. *What* about Ray Milland, then?'

145

'Wasn't it extraordinary how different he looked – not just being older, but having lost his hair like that. If it hadn't been for the cast-list I really don't think I'd have believed it was him!'

'Sad. He used to be so gorgeous – do you remember *Lost Weekend*?'

'Oh well, we're all a bit battered by Time now.'

'Yes. Thank God we don't lose our hair like men do. Robert's lucky, he's kept his very well, but Peter was getting a bit thin on top.'

'Yes, and Robert's kept his figure too – I wish I could say the same,' Betty sighed.

'Well – he's on the go all the time, think of all the calories he burns up!'

'This summer,' Betty said, 'I'm *really* going to do a proper diet – nothing but lettuce leaves and fruit juice, and lots of exercise. Perhaps I'll take up badminton with Tony and I could get an exercise bicycle . . . '

'You said just the same thing last year,' I reminded her unkindly.

Chapter Thirteen

The next day I reapplied myself to my work with especial vigour. I decided to put Gwen Richmond's murder right out of my mind and get on with what was, after all, my main purpose in being in Oxford. I was scribbling away energetically at my notes when I felt a light touch on my shoulder. It was Bill Howard whom I hadn't noticed sitting down in the next seat.

'Hi! Sorry to disturb you when you were working away with such concentration, but I just wanted to know if you and Michael would prefer French or Italian food tomorrow evening?'

'Oh, how lovely. Well, Italian would be nice.'

'Is there anywhere special you'd like to go – you probably know the restaurants here better than I do.'

'I believe the Murano in the High is supposed to be pretty good.'

'OK, then, I'll book a table for eight o'clock – will that be all right?'

'*Marvellous*. We'll look forward to it.'

I reflected, as I bent over my notes once more, that even if Dino Torcello wasn't our murderer, it would still be interesting to see what sort of restaurant he had created. I hoped that the food *would* be good since I had recommended it. I had the feeling that Bill Howard, if not actually a Foodie, cared more than most men about what precisely he ate and drank.

As I packed up my notebooks at the end of the

day I felt that particular glow of satisfaction you get when you know you've done a good day's work. There's nothing else quite like it in the world and I suppose it's the real reason why you go on slogging away when what your friends are doing seems much more agreeable and entertaining. I was just collecting my coat from the pegs outside Room 45 when Tony came up.

'I'm so glad I caught you – I've got a meeting this evening and I wanted to tell you straight away. I've remembered why I know Dino Torcello's name.'

'Really?'

'When we have a reception or some kind of 'do' on here, it's his restaurant that does the catering.'

'No!'

'*And* I've just been checking. There was a reception the evening that Gwen Richmond died. I remember now – there was a lot of kerfuffle with the police being around. Anyhow the reception *did* take place – for some librarians from Minneapolis – and the Torcello restaurants did all the canapés and things.'

'And they had to be delivered by somebody and that might just have been Dino!'

'He'd have come in round the back at the staff entrance – he'd have been expected – and delivered the food. Then he could easily have hidden – in one of the 'gents' – and come out when everything was quiet and found Gwen and killed her.'

'Could he have found out where Gwen was?'

'I suppose he could have asked, quite casually – people wouldn't take much notice. Anyway, I can ask around and see if anyone remembers.'

We looked at each other with some excitement.

'It *is* a possibility,' I said. 'He does have a pretty good motive. Anyway, Michael and I are being taken to dinner at the Murano tomorrow by Bill Howard, so perhaps I may see him.'

Michael *was* wearing a tie when I went to pick him

up the following evening and looked quite respectable. And although we had our usual disagreement about the necessity of polishing shoes, I was grateful that he wasn't wearing a pair of shabby old trainers, so I didn't press the matter.

The Murano was obviously one of Oxford's more fashionable restaurants. Apart from the prices (which were astronomical and made me feel rather guilty about having suggested it) the décor was very plush, with murals of Venetian lagoons and glass-blowing (all very atmospheric), the inevitable pink tablecloths and intimidating waiters. It was very full and, as is often the case in such places, the proprietor had crowded in too many tables and other people's conversations occasionally overlapped with ours.

I looked carefully at the head waiter who ushered us to our seats, whisked (pink) table napkins on to our laps and thrust giant leather-covered menus into our hands. He was too young to be Dino Torcello himself, but he was dark and looked definitely Italian so I felt safe in assuming that he was one of the sons.

'Well,' I said brightly, 'this *is* nice!'

Michael looked at me quizzically but Bill Howard said warmly, 'I'm so glad you were both able to come. I feel rather guilty, though, at dragging Michael away from whatever assignment he should be doing.'

'Oh I'm just faffing about – going round in circles a bit now – you know how it is when the exams are quite close. There's so much you feel you haven't done it hardly seems worth while doing anything!'

'Michael! That's *not*— '

'You probably know more than you think you do,' Bill broke in soothingly. 'That's what I used to find with my students – the ones who were bright anyway – and I'm sure Michael here is bright.'

A young waiter came and hovered over us and we applied ourselves to the menu.

'I'll have the parma ham and melon and then the osso bucco,' I said.

'*Fritto misto* for me,' Bill said, 'and then the tagliatelle with ham in the wine and mushroom sauce.'

'Oh – yes – perhaps I'd rather have the tagliatelle.' I relapsed into my usual indecisiveness about choosing. 'It does sound rather nice . . . '

'What about you, Michael?' Bill asked.

'I'll have the squid and then the osso bucco. I expect my mother has told you how we poor scholars are kept in a permanent state of starvation – it's a great treat to have real *food* instead of the cardboard substitutes one gets in Hall.'

'But surely college catering is supposed to be wonderful – and all those fine wines they lay down.'

'Only for the High Table. We poor serfs exist on gruel and water while the dons live it up with port and pheasant. It has always been so – you may recall Parson Woodforde.'

The conversation ambled gently through seventeenth- and eighteenth-century literature while we ate our first course. When the osso bucco and tagliatelle were placed before us the man I had decided was one of the Torcellos appeared bearing one of those enormous pepper mills that seem to be the badge of office of all Italian head waiters. I hate having pepper ground over my food by someone else so I always wave them away on principle, even if I really want the pepper. Bill and Michael, however, submitted to the ritual. The Torcello son moved to the next table whose occupants, a man and a woman, seemed to be regular customers since they engaged him in conversation, which he graciously inclined his head to hear.

Out of a blur of words I heard the woman say, 'And how is your father? We were so sorry to hear about his accident.'

'Yes, a broken arm takes so long to mend when you are not young. And, alas, it is his right arm so that he is virtually helpless. It makes him – as you can imagine – very restless. Even at his age he always likes to run things here and now he cannot do anything.'

'I imagine he wouldn't be an easy patient,' the woman said laughingly.

'Indeed he is not. Fortunately he is still able to attend Council meetings and so forth and that takes up some of his energy, but we will all be glad when the plaster is off – it has been six weeks now – and we can all get back to normal!'

He bowed and went away to chivvy one of his under-lings.

I became aware that Bill Howard was asking me a question.

'Have you been to the performance of *All's Well* in Trinity College gardens?'

'Oh – I'm so sorry – no, not yet. I'm never lucky with the weather for anything out of doors. Do you remember your college production of *The Wasps*, Michael? When we all sat in a fine drizzle under umbrellas but still contrived to get bitten to pieces by mosquitoes!'

I continued to make conversation mechanically but I was greatly preoccupied with what I had just heard. If Dino Torcello – an elderly man now – had his right arm in plaster it seemed unlikely that he would have been able to summon up the strength to kill Gwen Richmond and pull a largish bookcase down on top of her. In any case, he obviously hadn't been allowed anywhere near his restaurants so he wouldn't have had an excuse to get into the Bodleian anyway. It seemed that every door I opened hopefully in this investigation was immediately slammed in my face. I pulled myself together and concentrated on the conversation. Bill and Michael were discussing Chekhov.

'They did the last act – where the girl, Nina, comes back – so well,' Bill was saying, 'you really did get the feel of what it must have been like in a second-rate touring company in Russia before the Revolution – great atmosphere.'

'I haven't seen this National Theatre production,' I said, 'but I love *The Seagull* – I think it's my favourite of all the Chekhov plays. I remember – years ago – being taken to see a production by the Moscow Arts Theatre. It was incredible – we didn't know any Russian, of course, but by the end we felt we'd understood every word!'

The waiter arrived with our zabagliones.

'My, this looks good!' Bill said, just like someone out of a film, which made Michael splutter slightly. I gave him a severe look.

It was a pleasant evening, relaxed and cosy and as we came out of the Murano and stood on the pavement while Bill finished off a story he had been telling about some extraordinary woman he'd met at a seminar, I felt peaceful and happy, in spite of my disappointment about Dino Torcello. Really, I told myself, it wouldn't be the end of the world if I *never* knew who killed Gwen Richmond.

A light rain began to fall and I felt in my bag for a scarf to tie over my hair. Bill Howard produced a tweed hat from the pocket of his Burberry and put it on. In the hat he looked quite different and much younger. He reminded me of someone but I couldn't think who.

'Can I get you a cab?' he asked.

'No, we're fine,' I said. 'I left my car outside Michael's college and it's not far. Thank you for a lovely evening.'

'It's been my pleasure.'

Michael added his thanks to mine and we parted on the corner of the Turl.

'Your chum in the CIA is quite fun,' Michael said as we negotiated the bollards half-way along the road.

'The CIA?' I said startled.

'That raincoat, with the collar turned up – all tall and broad-shouldered – you must agree, that's what he looks like.'

I laughed. 'You're right. I thought he reminded me of someone this evening – perhaps that was it!'

The next morning I told Tony about the collapse of our theory.

'Oh well, that's that, then,' he said. 'There really isn't anyone else. Perhaps it *was* an accident after all.'

'Perhaps.'

I took Robert and Betty and Tony out to dinner at the Torcello restaurant in Woodstock the following evening. There was no sign of an elderly Italian with his arm in plaster but the food was excellent and we all enjoyed ourselves. I also took Fitz, Elaine and Bill Howard out to dinner (to a rather grand Chinese place Fitz chose) and came away – as I so often used to do with Fitz in the old days – feeling rather downcast at my own lack of high seriousness or even moderate intelligence.

I had now more or less finished my work in the Bodleian. I was having a quick lunch with Tony – a sandwich and a glass of wine at the King's Arms – and told him that I just had a few things to check and then I could go back home and write my paper.

'Why don't you stay and write it here? We love having you, you know that. You're the best listener we ever have!'

'And I love being here. But I must get back to the animals – you know what it's like. As it is, Foss won't speak to me for days and the dogs will be thoroughly spoiled if they stay with Rosemary much longer. Anyway, I'll be coming back for the wedding.'

'Did you know that Mother's more or less taken over all the arrangements?'

'You don't surprise me in the least. I hope Pamela will be allowed to choose her own wedding dress at least.'

'Well . . . Mother *did* say that she was going up to London next week if Pamela felt like going with her to have a look round . . . '

We both laughed.

153

'Pamela and her mother don't seem to mind, thank goodness.'

'It would be like minding a force of nature! And, actually, it will obviously be easier for Betty to see to the reception and things – I expect most of the guests will be from your side.'

We discussed Tony's future plans for a while and then he looked at his watch and said, 'I must be off. I want to go down into the store and see about a few things.'

'You mean the underground bit – how fascinating.'

'Have you ever seen it?'

'No. I've always longed to.'

'Come with me, then, and I'll give you the guided tour. We'll start off in Duke Humfrey.'

We went through the arched doorway with its Latin inscription:

QUOD FELICITER VORTAT
ACADEMICI OXONIENS
BIBLIOTHECAM HANC
VOBIS REPUBLICAEQUE
LITERATORUM
T. B. P.

I found the wooden stairs steeper now than in the days when I had rushed up them so eagerly to see if Rupert was there. I stood in the library, under the great dark-beamed roof with its brilliantly coloured ceiling, looking at the gilt-framed portraits on the walls and felt again, as I always did, a little surge of gratitude that I should have been allowed to spend time in such a splendid place.

We walked between the tall shelves, light from the arched windows glowing on the rich leather bindings of the books, our footsteps echoing on the floor, passing through Arts End and up into the more modern section

154

until we found ourselves in a smallish room. In one corner was a sort of moving belt above which was a notice written in the minatory style that seems to come naturally to librarians:

Before loading books into the elevator ensure that the books are distributed as evenly as possible across the width of the box.

'Goodness,' I said, 'whatever is this?'

'Oh, that's our pride and joy,' Tony said, 'the book conveyor. It takes books from one building to another on a sort of conveyor-belt system.'

'Underground?'

'Oh yes – from Duke Humfrey and the Upper Reading Room to the New Bodleian.'

'You mean, it's all going on under the Broad?'

'Sure. Come on we'll go down into the basement.'

Tony unlocked the door ('We have to be pretty hot on security!') and we got into a small lift and went down into what seemed like the bowels of the earth. After walking along a tunnel we found ourselves in one of the many bookstores.

'I thought you might like to see these particular sliding bookcases,' Tony said. 'They were invented by Mr Gladstone.' He demonstrated one. 'Neat aren't they? He wrote a study called *Books and their Housing* – he'd have made a good librarian.'

I was peering (as I always do) at the book shelves and found that these particular ones contained a collection of 1920s girls' school stories. 'Oh look! Elinor Brent Dyer – all the Chalet School books! There are some here I've never seen anywhere before. How marvellous!'

'You must come in one day and have a good read.'

'Yes. One always forgets that the Bodleian has treasures like these as well as all the *old* books!'

'People come in and read Mills and Boon and some-times back copies of *Woman's Weekly*. You must remem-ber that we're a copyright library – which is why we're rapidly running out of space. It's a bit like *Alice* – running as hard as you can just to stay in the same spot.'

We turned back and walked along the rather dismal passages with pipes overhead and the continual hum of air conditioning and the clatter of the book conveyor which flowed along beside us like a noisy river.

'However far down are we?' I asked, as we continued down a sloping tunnel.

'Well there are three floors below ground. And here we are in the New Library. Will you hang on for a minute. I just want to have a word with Bernard . . .'

He disappeared round a corner of some bookcases and I went on looking about me. There were books everywhere of course, on many different kinds of shelving and some in wire cages as if they were dangerous animals. There were book trolleys of various ingenious shapes and even what appeared to be a supermarket trolley, though I thought it unlikely that a member of the Bodleian staff had actually walked away with one from Sainsbury's! I wandered over to a table with a notice which said: '*Do not place anything on this table*' and another whose notice sternly admonished: '*On no account are any books on this table to be removed*' and I reflected with some amuse-ment that prohibition seemed to be the natural mode of expression of those who worked in libraries. Anyway, I have always felt that all librarians bitterly resent any-one removing books from the shelves – where they each occupy their especial space in their own well-ordered habitat – and actually *reading* them.

Tony reappeared quite suddenly and I was reminded (because of the underground tunnels, I suppose) of the White Rabbit.

'Isn't it fun!' I said. 'You are so lucky to work here!'

Tony smiled at me indulgently and I reflected sadly, not

for the first time, that the young today seem unacquainted with the joys of frivolity. I assumed a more serious expression.

'How many books are there down here?'

'I can't give you an accurate figure – but it's about sixty per cent of the storage capacity of the building.'

'Good heavens! Just books – well books and journals, I suppose?'

'Mostly. Though one of Bodley's librarians in the nineteen thirties had a thing about ephemera, so somewhere – I don't know precisely where – there are boxes full of bus tickets, grocers' bags and old handbills.'

'How lovely!'

He smiled again in recognition of my enthusiasm for trivia.

We went through more passages festooned with pipes and firebox switches, lit by bare bulbs dangling from cords – I thought of the richness of Duke Humfrey and the soaring circular glory of the Radcliffe Camera up above – and got in another rather cramped lift from which we emerged into the familiar corridors of the New Bodleian just by Room 45.

'Oh, thank you, Tony,' I said, 'that was fascinating. I feel really privileged!'

'Well, as a matter of fact we do what we call extended tours quite frequently – you could have gone on one of those – it would have been more informative than I was. It does the whole thing – Duke Humfrey, the Radcliffe Camera and the underground store – the works.'

'I think it was cosier going round with you,' I said and went into Room 45 to check through a few final things for my notes.

It was about teatime when I emerged and I stood for a moment savouring the nostalgia that this time of day in Oxford always gives me. It's stronger, of course, in the winter term when you come out into the dusk, but even in broad daylight the feeling is there. For a few moments I was an undergraduate again, an afternoon's work behind me, about to go back to my room in college to toast crumpets or perhaps go out to tea – I could see the look of concentration on Rupert's face as he carefully cut into the Fuller's walnut cake so that the white icing didn't crumble. I was so lost in memories that I was half-way down Parks Road before I realised that I hadn't collected my shopping bag from the desk at Duke Humfrey and had to go all the way back for it.

Chapter Fourteen

The sun was really hot as I drove into Oxford the next morning. I switched on a tape of some Elizabethan music and thought how nice it would be to go a'maying – whatever that might involve. If the weather went on like this I might drive back to Taviscombe by way of Stratford. The gardens at New Place and Hall Croft (one of my favourite places in the whole world) would be beautiful now.

As I walked down the narrow lane into the Parks I wondered if I might see Fitz. Sure enough, as I crossed the grass I saw his tall figure walking towards one of the seats under the trees. I watched him with some amusement. The stick certainly *was* for effect since he wasn't leaning on it but, on the contrary, twirling it in a rather dashing way as he walked quite briskly without its aid. Pippa was following close at his heels, making occasional little forays in various directions as some new smell caught her attention. They looked, as I'm sure Fitz intended, the perfect archetypal picture of a distinguished elderly gentleman and his dog Out For A Walk.

I waited until he was settled on his seat and then approached.

'Hello Fitz,' I said, 'isn't it a glorious day.'

'Ah, Chloe.'

It seemed to me that Fitz was displeased for some reason, but I persevered.

'No cricket today?'

159

'As you see.'

The monosyllabic reply and the fact that he didn't invite me to join him on the seat indicated that he was definitely put out about something. I was curious to find out what it was so I sat down beside him, bending forward to stroke Pippa's head. There was a brief silence and then Fitz said, 'Bill Howard tells me that you are playing at detectives.'

So that was it.

'Yes,' I said, immediately on the defensive, as I so often was with Fitz.

'I would have thought that such things were more properly left to the police, who are presumably qualified to deal with them.'

'But, you see, they thought that it was an accident – it was only after Tony told me about how he found her that I realised that they hadn't had all the facts and couldn't have made a proper judgement.'

'And why should you feel that *you* were obliged to do their investigating for them?'

'Poor Tony was very upset . . . '

'I can only suppose,' he said distastefully, 'that you have lived for too long in a dreary seaside town where the only form of mental stimulus is vulgar curiosity about one's neighbours' affairs. I had not thought you would have sunk to such a level of existence.'

Fitz in his supercilious mood had always made me feel angry and resentful.

'It *wasn't* vulgar curiosity,' I said. I always sounded like a petulant child when I was arguing with him. 'I just wanted to help. The police had missed certain things – I thought if I tried to piece things together . . . '

He gave a short laugh.

> 'Here after ignorance, instruction speaks;
> Here, clarity of candour, history's soul,
> The critical mind, in short; no gossip-guess.'

I groaned inwardly. When Fitz began quoting *The Ring and the Book* it meant that he was at his most difficult and opinionated, capable of pursuing a subject to death simply to show off his superiority in argument.

'Well, why not?' I asked defiantly. 'Don't you think I am capable of connected reasoning?'

'To be honest, no. It has, indeed, always been a source of sorrow to me that your work – especially that essay on George Eliot – was marred by a lack of lucidity. You rely too much – wholly, perhaps – upon a purely subjective approach to your subject – what our American friends call "a gut reaction", I believe. The intellectual content seems to me to be largely lacking. This might be forgivable, perhaps, in a *young*, over-enthusiastic female undergraduate, but it is unfortunate, to say the least, in a person of mature years with some pretensions to a critical approach to English literature. How, I ask myself, could *you* expect to achieve the "patent-truth-extracting-process" as the Master calls it.'

It was one of his affectations always to refer to Browning and not Henry James as the Master, something that has always irritated me. Although I'm not one of those self-assured critics who believe that everything I write has the authority of words handed down directly from Mount Sinai (indeed, like many of my age and sex, I tend to suffer from a positive lack of self-confidence) I am still upset and offended if anyone makes derogatory remarks about my work.

'All right, so I know I'm not an *academic* like you,' I poured all the scorn I could muster into the word, 'but the very fact that *I* haven't been living in an ivory tower for the past fifty odd years but have had to battle my way in the real world, where people actually live and *suffer* may have made me a little more responsive to works of literature that were written by *real* people than you are!'

He made no reply but tilted his head back in an

attitude of arrogant enquiry which so infuriated me that I burst out, 'Anyway, poor wretched Gwen Richmond has some rights, and if she was murdered (and I'm sure she was) then I don't want to see her killer going free.'

As I spoke Gwen Richmond's name he stiffened.

'You will oblige me by not mentioning that creature's name . . . '

'Yes,' I said placatingly, 'I know about Lance and how she hurt you – you and Elaine – and I'm very sorry for you both, it must have been terrible. But, even so, she didn't deserve to be killed, she had the right to live.'

I paused, slightly fearful of what I had said, and there was a moment's silence.

'She had no right to live.' He dropped the words like slivers of ice into the silence.

'For God's sake, Fitz . . . '

'She ruined two lives and destroyed a third, how could the God you invoke have allowed her to live so long. She was an old woman when she died. He – he was scarcely more than a boy – all his life and work before him, before us all. She was vicious and without principles . . . '

'But she loved him.'

'*Love!*' He spat out the word as if it was something unspeakable. 'What did *she* know about love – lust, perhaps, and ambition and greed. What do any of you know about real love?'

'I know about love,' I said. 'I too have lost someone I cared about very much, so I do know how you must have felt.'

'There is no comparison. Lance was someone special, he would have been a great writer – his loss was immeasurable.'

I was seized with a furious rage. How dare Fitz imply that Peter's life, all the things he had achieved, all the love that he had given to Michael and to me, were of no account. I lashed out.

'Well, certainly *you* had a motive for killing her – by your own admission a far bigger motive than anyone else.'

'I could not have killed her.' The reply was stiff and formal.

'Oh, I know you were supposed to be in Duke Humfrey that afternoon, but— ' A thought struck me, of such overwhelming significance that I rushed on more in excitement now than anger. 'But there *was* a way you could have done it, giving yourself an alibi in Duke Humfrey – making a great fuss about some books so that everyone would remember seeing you – and still have got to Room 45 without going past George at the desk. You could have joined one of those extended tours – I bet there was one that day – and gone through the underground store and then, when you came up in the New Bodleian you could have slipped away, found Gwen and killed her. Then all you would have had to do was walk casually past when George was occupied with someone coming in – he doesn't notice people going *out*, any more than the man on the desk in Duke Humfrey does. It would have been easy.'

I paused for a moment to see how Fitz was reacting, but his face was like stone with no vestige of emotion. I went on.

'You were physically capable of killing her. You are tall and quite vigorous for your age – in spite of that walking stick – and she was small and frail and sitting down, taken by surprise, no doubt by your sudden appearance – though, even after all these years she would have known at once who you were. I don't know *how* you meant to kill her – but the fact that you planned it all with so much care means that that was in your mind, but I think the actual killing didn't happen as you intended. What I imagine happened was that you spelled out to her, as you have to me, the enormity of her crime and she protested – that she loved Lance, that her grief had been as great as yours. This would have been intolerable to you and so you snatched up that large, metal-bound book and hit out at her and killed her. When you saw what you had done, you knew you must make it look like an accident, so you arranged the body and the ladder and then loosened the screws – with a paperknife, perhaps, there was one there, Tony says – and brought the shelves down on top of her. And that's how you killed Gwen Richmond.'

I found I was breathless, partly from my long speech and partly from excitement as I fitted each possibility into place. There was no doubt in my mind that I had solved the mystery of Gwen Richmond's death and I felt as triumphant as if I had solved a fiendishly difficult crossword puzzle.

I turned to face Fitz and was brought up short by his look of cold contempt.

'Have you finished expounding your theories?'

I was silent.

'I see I must make my meaning plainer for you to understand. When I said I could not have killed her, I meant that such an act would be impossible for me. To kill her would have been to recognise her existence, to admit that she had any part at all in Lance's life.' His voice was unsteady as he spoke the name. 'She was merely an instrument – vile and without meaning in itself – of his death. He was killed because in a moment of weakness he chose to move out into another world, where we could not protect him, a world full of mean and unworthy creatures, like that woman, who would debase his talent and eat away at his love for us. In the beginning,' he went on, a note of self-distaste in his voice, 'I thought that she was a harmless creature, someone who would entertain Elaine, even amuse me. But, of course, it was all deception and treachery. We learned, Elaine and I, the hard way, not to trust anyone again.'

He paused and I sat silently, confused and unhappy. Then he continued sardonically. 'If, however, you merely wish me to establish an alibi – is that what you investigators call it? – then perhaps the testimony of the Hobbes Professor of Moral Philosophy will do. I left Duke Humfrey with him just after two-thirty. And if that is not sufficient, we may add the names of Professor Gilbertson, Dr Montgomery and the Dean of Wadham. We were attending a meeting in All Souls – about an exhibition at the Casa Guidi in Florence next year, if that is relevant.'

I sat submissively while his scornful voice went remorselessly on. When he had finished there was silence again, a long silence, heavy with unspoken words. I somehow found the courage to speak.

'Fitz . . . I don't know what to say. I'm sorry. You made me angry – I got carried away by a stupid theory and didn't think . . . '

'That is what I have been complaining about.' Again the icy contempt. 'You do not think. You go plunging about in a mindless way, blundering through people's lives with no thought for those very feelings that you are so anxious to lay claim to yourself. You open up barely healed wounds, challenge the memory to face things that have been carefully hidden away for nearly a lifetime – and all for what? So that you can indulge yourself with a sort of game, a superior kind of acrostic, so that you can fancy yourself cleverer than your fellow creatures by reason of your *deductions*. You are despicable.'

There was nothing I could say. So much of what he had said was true. I had been carried away by my 'theory' to such an extent that I hadn't stopped to consider the people involved. Of course Fitz couldn't have killed Gwen. I had exonerated Freda Lassiter simply on instinct. How much worse was it to have accused Fitz (even in my mind, let alone to his face like this) who I knew so well. It would not be virtue or compassion that would stop him but a kind of fastidiousness that would never allow him to commit such an act. And I had hurt

165

him deeply. I had lost an old friend, for I knew that he would never forgive me for what I had said.

His next words seemed to confirm this.

'Since it is unlikely that we will ever meet again,' he said, and now there was malice in his voice, 'there is something I feel you should know.'

I looked at him without speaking.

'It is about Rupert.'

'Rupert!'

I felt a sudden cold premonition – I knew that he was going to say something I couldn't bear to hear.

'Do you remember that last summer? You had just gone down, Rupert was coming to spend some time with you and your mother at Taviscombe, but he had to cancel it at the last minute.'

'Yes. He had to go to Italy with his parents.'

'Not with his parents. With me.'

'With you?' I said uncomprehendingly.

'We were lovers of course,' Fitz said casually. 'But Rupert was a conventional boy and his parents were *very* conventional. His father, as you know, was a judge, so Rupert felt the need to be extra careful – the law, you may remember, at that time was not *kind*. So it seemed expedient that he should be seen to have a "girlfriend".' He put contemptuous inverted commas round the phrase.

'And that my dear Chloe is where you came in – especially, of course, when his parents visited him and you were carefully trotted out.'

I had a sudden vivid memory of sitting nervously in the Randolph at a family lunch party with Sir Frederick and Lady Drummond. He had a booming voice and an overbearing manner, but was basically kind; she was fashionable and sharp-eyed and did not approve of me at all.

Fitz was speaking again.

'You were so amazingly naïve! I couldn't believe it at first, but you actually believed that Rupert was in

166

love with you and that I – I was a charming friend!'

It is true. I was naïve. It seems incredible to imagine now, but in those days I (and most of the girls I knew) barely realised that such relationships existed. Oscar Wilde we knew about, of course, and that that sort of thing was against the law. I remember, when I was about sixteen, describing a friend of ours as a bit queer, and how my brother Jeremy took me to one side and explained why I mustn't use that particular phrase. I was astonished – not at the word's double meaning, but because it had never occurred to me that anyone one actually *knew* might be described in such a way.

Of course, it explained so much about Rupert – the elaborate and extravagant phrases and the chaste kisses – the idea of love was cleverly planted in my mind, and I was so willing to believe him, so besotted by his charm and beauty that I eagerly accepted the base coin that he offered as pure gold.

'You must have wondered,' Fitz said spitefully, 'what on earth Rupert could possibly have seen in *you* when he might have had his pick of any of the really beautiful or intelligent girls around. But, of course, *they* would have discovered very soon where his predilections lay. Only sweet, simple Chloe . . . You were a constant source of amazement and delight to us, my dear, we could not believe that you were true.'

I sat rigid, icy cold, unable to move or speak.

'The letter you wrote to me when he died,' the remorseless voice went on, 'I felt that perhaps I should have told you then – but it would have been too cruel, would it not? Cruel,' he repeated harshly. I heard the pain behind the malice. Perhaps I deserved it – pain for pain.

'It seemed to us incredible that you never solved *our* little deception when you had such a splendid clue.'

I looked at him blankly.

'Why your very own namesake, my dear, the poet Prior – no relation we always felt – what did he *almost* say:

167

The merchant to secure his treasure,
Conveys it in a borrowed name:
Chloe serves to grace my measure:
But Fitz, he is my real flame.'

He got up rather stiffly from the seat, raised his hat and bowed.

'Goodbye – Chloe.'

I don't know how long I sat there. I was so overwhelmed with hurt and humiliation that for a while I simply couldn't focus on the world around me. My eyes were blurred with tears of rage and shame at my own folly. Then came the dreadful sense of loss.

After a while I became aware of a movement close by. A small white dog had run up to me and dropped a stick at my feet. Automatically I bent to pick it up and standing up I threw it with all my strength as far as I could. The dog ran after it barking excitedly.

Now that I was on my feet, I moved slowly away from the seat and across the grass. I walked slowly because I felt weak, as if I was recovering from a long illness. People passed me but they seemed to have no substance. They were like shadows cast by the sun that blazed down as I trudged on in a sort of daze. Only when I was outside the Parks did some of the numbness wear off. I stood staring at the great horse chestnut tree outside the Clarendon Laboratory, deliberately forcing myself to concentrate on the white blossoms, trying to pick out each particular flower head.

There was a lot of movement around me now – young men and women, students coming out of lectures. I became aware that one young man, his arms full of books and folders, had stopped and was looking at me strangely.

'For God's sake, Ma,' Michael said, 'whatever's the matter? You look terrible.'

I made an immense effort and attempted a bright smile.

'I was just looking at that marvellous tree,' I said. My voice sounded blurred and unreal.

Michael shifted his books and took my arm.

'Come on,' he said, 'I'll make you a cup of coffee.'

Chapter Fifteen

I took a sip of the very strong coffee that Michael had made. With some vague idea of treating me for shock he had put in several spoonfuls of sugar and it tasted disgusting, but, in a way, comforting. It was, after all, tangible proof that someone cared.

Michael had been tactfully silent on the way back to his college, but now he said, 'Can you tell me what happened?'

'It was Fitz,' I said.

I knew that I could only tell Michael part of what had happened. Everything that concerned Rupert would have to be hidden away, for many years perhaps, until the passage of time had made it bearable to look at. I explained how I had put my 'theory' to Fitz and how hurt and angry he was.

'Still,' Michael said, 'he had no right to upset you like that.'

'He was my friend and I accused him of murder. I opened up old wounds. It *was* unforgivable.'

I cautiously drank a little more of my coffee.

'Well,' Michael said uncertainly, 'I still think he was pretty rotten to you. Anyway,' he continued briskly, 'if he wasn't the murderer who *was* it?'

'Oh, no,' I said, 'that's it. I don't intend to speculate any more. I've meddled enough – I've learnt my lesson.'

'But—'

170

'No!'

'OK.' Michael got up from the floor where he had been sitting surrounded by a pile of old examination papers. 'Let's go and have some lunch.'

'No, love, it's all right. I'm quite OK now. I've taken up too much of your time as it is. You must do some work.'

'I've got to *eat*, haven't I? Anyway I sat up until four o'clock this morning trying to polish off the Hapsburg Empire so I deserve a little break. Are you going to finish that coffee?'

'It was delicious – but no, I don't think so.'

He laughed and put the cup on to a rather nice Portmeirion tray that I hadn't seen before.

'That's pretty,' I said. 'Where did you get it?'

'Rachel gave it to me?'

'Who's Rachel?'

Michael laughed again.

'I'm glad to see you're your old inquisitive self again! She's just a girl.'

While I was considering the implications of girls who gave him elegant teatrays, Michael had got his jacket.

'I know,' he said, 'let's go to the Falkland Arms at Great Tew. They'll have their new guest beer in for this week.'

'It's quite a way,' I said doubtfully, 'you really ought to be working.'

'Oh, Ma, don't *fuss*. Tell you what, I can use it as driving practice.'

I had been paying for him to have driving lessons as a bribe to make him give up the motor bike, which I had been persuaded, against my better judgement, to let him have when he first went up to Oxford. Occasionally we went out together for a little driving practice, but it was not an experience I actively enjoyed.

'Anyway,' he said, 'you oughtn't to drive straight after you've had a shock. Are the L plates in the boot?'

He swept me out of the room and across the quadrangle before I could protest. Going to the car we didn't walk back through the Parks but took the long way round.

On the way to Great Tew my mind was too occupied with worrying about Michael's driving (which was quite good, really, if a little fast) to allow me to brood on what had happened that morning. I suddenly realised that that was Michael's intention and I smiled at him affectionately.

'That's better, Ma. You're relaxing a little, your knuckles aren't white with grasping the seat belt in terror at my driving.'

'Idiot boy! Careful! You're much too close in to the side of the road!'

Even though we were quite early, the Falkland Arms was crowded. Michael studied the blackboard behind the bar.

'You're going to have to drive back because they've got Jennings *and* Burtonwood this week and I'll have to try them both. So what will you have?'

'I'll have a spritzer then.'

'Get you!'

I went and sat on an oak settle by the old open fireplace where one of the two pub cats was already stretched out. Michael put our glasses down on the small round table.

'There's your yuppie drink.'

'Do you know,' I said, 'I suddenly realised the other day, that even if I could *afford* a Porsche, I'd be too old and stiff to get inside it.'

'You poor old thing!'

He held up his glass and regarded the beer.

'This isn't bad – I might have the other half. And no – it will not impair my intellectual faculties and stop me working this afternoon.'

'I didn't say a thing!'

'You have ways of *not* saying things that are more

172

vehement than the most forthright statement. What shall we have – food or sandwiches?'

'Oh, proper food, I think. You need feeding up and, anyway, sandwiches aren't really safe with these cats around.'

The pub cats had a splendid party trick. They would sit peacefully beside you until your sandwich arrived and then, just as you were lifting it from the plate, a paw would flash out and, with one deft movement, the meat would be whisked away and you would be left holding two pieces of bread. Foolish people like me sometimes bought sandwiches specially to see them do it.

After our lunch we strolled up past the pub to look at the newly thatched and restored houses.

'Very fancy,' Michael said. 'But, I must say, I preferred the place when they were romantic ruins. No atmosphere of the past – which reminds me, if I'm going to be sitting up till all hours brooding over Franz-Joseph and the Serbo-Bosnian question, I'll need some more milk – I think they'll have some in the shop here.'

The little shop was empty except for a woman buying stamps at the post-office counter. As she picked up her change and came towards the door I saw that it was Molly Richmond. My first instinct was to turn away – the last thing I wanted today was to be reminded of Gwen Richmond. But she had seen me and greeted me with an exclamation of pleasure. I introduced Michael and we chatted casually for a few moments and then she said, 'It's really quite a coincidence, our meeting, because I was going to write to you. I've found the other notebook – you know, the remainder of Gwen's diary. I thought you might like to have a look at it. I know how useful you said the other one would be for your work.'

'My work . . .'

'Your article on wartime writers. Would you like to come back with me now and I can let you have it.'

Trying to hide my reluctance, I said, 'How kind –
that would be splendid.'

'I'm sorry I can't ask you in for a cup of coffee,'
Molly said as we walked down the hill towards Tithings
Cottage, 'but today's my embroidery class – we meet in
the Village Hall twice a week. I'm doing a set of chair
seats – *gros point*, you know – a Victorian design I took
from some de Morgan tiles. Gwen was *very* scornful about
them. How strange,' she stopped to open the gate, 'I was
actually at my class when Gwen died. I came back to find
a young policeman on the doorstep, who had come to tell
me about the accident.'

Michael's eyes met mine. Another door – the final
one – shut in my face and I felt only relief that it was
all over.

When we got back to the car I threw the notebook
into my shopping bag.

'Aren't you going to look at it?' Michael asked.

'No – not today, anyway.'

'Pity. It might have the answer to the whole mystery.'

'It can stay a mystery as far as I'm concerned,' I said,
and for the rest of the drive back I talked resolutely of
other things.

When I got back to Woodstock I found Betty stuffing
clothes into a black plastic dustbin bag.

'Oxfam,' she said in response to my enquiry. She
picked up a pair of shoes. 'They were perfectly all
right for the first few times I wore them and then they
turned against me and now they're agony. I really can't
understand it.'

She put them to one side and began sorting through
some blouses.

I suddenly said, 'Hang on,' and ran upstairs. I took out
of the wardrobe the new skirt I'd bought to go to dinner
with Fitz and Elaine and went downstairs with it.

'Here you are,' I said, 'bung this in.'

'But you've only just bought it,' Betty protested.

'Yes, well, I didn't feel right in it,' I said and rolled it up and thrust it deep into the bag.

I went to bed early that evening saying I felt tired, and, indeed, I felt exhausted after the events of the day. I picked up my shopping bag to put it ready for the morning and saw Gwen Richmond's notebook. I took it out and looked at it. It was the same sort of hard-covered notebook as the other, though dark blue where the first one had been dark red. Almost against my will I opened it. There weren't very many entries. I sat down on the bed and began to read.

Thursday. May told me that she'd seen Johnny, her young man, and done what I'd said – about the black-market deals, that is. He said he needed time to think and said he'd meet her by the stile at Hanger Wood when he gets off duty tomorrow night, about 10.30. I don't know if she's got the guts to carry it off. He might try and bully her, she's pretty feeble. I think I'll go along too – I won't tell her. If I hide behind the hedge by the stile they won't notice me but I should be able to hear what's going on and back her up if he goes on trying to wriggle out of things. I must say I don't feel much like wandering about the countryside in the dark at the moment. I think I've got a cold or flu or something coming on, I'm sure I've got a temperature. But I'm damned if that bastard's going to get away with things like that. May is pretty dim but that's no reason why that swine of a man should make her get rid of the baby if she doesn't want to, and she's obviously petrified of telling her father.

Friday. I really do feel terrible and it's not just this fever, whatever it is. The most terrible thing's happened. I got to the wood about 10.15, before May, and found a place behind the hedge. I was

175

pretty sure I could hear all right from there and the branches were fairly thin so that, when my eyes got used to the darkness, I could just about see as well. May arrived and stood by the side of the road and after a bit I heard a car coming. May stepped forward, but instead of stopping, the car – actually it was a jeep – drove straight at her. There's no doubt in my mind that the driver did it deliberately. I was rooted to the spot for a moment, and then, before I could go and see how badly hurt May was, the driver got out of the jeep. He went back to where she was lying and shone a torch on her. He lifted her head and then let it drop. It fell with a thud on the road and I knew that she must be dead. Then he got back into the jeep and drove away. In the light of the torch I saw who he was. It was the one she called James Mason. After a bit I crept out from behind the hedge and went to look at May. I hadn't got a torch but I felt for her pulse and she was dead all right. I had to leave her there. I don't want to be involved and if they think it was an accident then no one will know about the baby. I'm sure that's what she would have wanted. Anyway, if I say I was on the spot when it happened then it will be a great hassle and I can do without that. But I'm damned sure I'm not going to let that man get away with it. I'll go and see him and let him know that I saw him – I can threaten to go to the authorities and make his life pretty good Hell – a sort of rough justice. Tomorrow will be dreadful when the Browns find out about May. I can't write any more, I really do feel rough.

Saturday. All hell has broken loose here today as I expected, but they seem to have decided that it was an accident and the driver just didn't see her – there've been a lot of accidents lately in the dark nights now people can't have proper headlights. No wonder I've felt so awful – they had to get the doctor for me and he says I've got chicken pox!

Wednesday. Haven't been able to write anything for over a week now, but feel better today. In a few days, when I'm allowed out again I must go up to the airfield and see if I can find the James Mason man.

Saturday. They've gone! All of them – aircraft and all. Ray Burton in the village says that they've been moved down to the south coast – apparently there's something big about to happen and everything's being concentrated down there – perhaps it's the Second Front at last. So there's nothing I can do about the man who killed May – he's got away with it. And the one who got her pregnant, the one she called Johnny. Life's bloody unfair when you think about it. I must get out of this place – it's really getting me down. Brown is more silent and surly than ever now that May's dead and Mrs B. is always crying. I've applied for the WAAF – I must see who can pull a few strings for me. Sick of this diary, too . . .

And there the diary entries finished and the rest of the notebook was empty. Except, as I flicked over the pages a snapshot fell out. It was brownish and rather creased and on the back was written in uneven capitals: 'ME WITH JOHNNY AND CHUCK'. The photograph showed a young girl with shoulder-length hair done up in a snood. She was wearing a short fur-fabric jacket and a tight skirt and a lot of dark lipstick. She had her arms round two young men. One had dark hair, and was flashily good looking, the other certainly did look like James Mason.

I looked at the photograph and knew immediately that there was one important factor that I simply hadn't realised, one thing that made the whole thing quite plain.

Now that I had the information I didn't know what I was going to do with it.

The next morning – my last day in Oxford – I left the house early, saying that I wanted to be sure of getting a parking space.

'I can't think why you don't go to the Pear Tree car park like I do,' said Betty who was cutting up some heart for Cleopatra, 'and then go in on the Park and Ride.'

'Yes, it is silly, I suppose,' I agreed idly, stroking Cleopatra as she sat on the work-top impatiently watching the progress of her breakfast. 'Anyway, I'll be off now. I don't expect to be late this evening. I've booked a table at the Bell in Charlbury for us all. Is eight o'clock OK?'

But when I got into the car I didn't turn in the direction of Oxford, instead I drove out of Woodstock towards North Leigh and parked by a gate beside a wood. A sign by the gate said 'ROMAN VILLA' and as I went down the steep track with fields on either side, a tractor came up from the valley past me and the driver called out 'Good morning' and I waved in response. Half-way along the path I stopped and looked down at the outline of a small Roman villa laid out below. The sun was bright and the birds were singing their hearts out and I hoped very much that the people who built the villa had also seen such days when the warmth of the sun and the blueness of the sky might have made grey barbaric Britain seem a more agreeable place of exile.

It was early and the custodian of the place had not yet arrived, so I opened the gate and went in and sat on a largish piece of masonry. I loved it here – the countryside around was beautiful and there was a wonderful atmosphere about the place itself, a feeling of the continuity of human life and experience, and, somehow, a sort of comfort. Perhaps, I thought, the Lares and Penates were still here, guiding and protecting those who came to look for them.

I had said that I didn't want to meddle any more in

Gwen Richmond's death. It was nothing to do with me. No one had asked me to investigate it. I had no right to interfere in people's lives – I had already caused enough unhappiness and anger. I thought of Peter Wimsey agonising, at the end of *Busman's Honeymoon*, about the execution of Frank Crutchley. At least I didn't have to face the possibility of sending someone to the gallows. But still – if the police believed me – the murderer would be shut away in some terrible prison for many years and that might be even worse. But now I was considering not just Gwen Richmond's death, but that of poor little May Brown and her unborn baby. A skylark was singing overhead, soaring against the sun, small, perfect, joyful. May's child had never been allowed to see a skylark. Perhaps it was just a stupid sentimental thought but it decided me. I got up and walked slowly back to the car. In Stonesfield I found a telephone box and made two calls. Then I drove into Oxford.

Chapter Sixteen

I love the Eagle and Child. I like to think of Tolkien, C. S. Lewis and Charles Williams getting together over a manly tankard of beer, engaged in literary talk like 1930s *belles-lettres*. The Bird and the Baby they called it, I believe, though I would not be so familiar myself. It was before twelve o'clock when I arrived and there were very few people there. I went to the bar and got two gin and tonics and settled down in one of the small alcoves just by the door.

When Bill Howard arrived I said, 'I've got you a gin and tonic, is that all right?'

He looked slightly surprised but said, 'Sure, that's fine.'

He sat down and poured some of the tonic into his gin.

'Well, what's it all about? You said it was urgent.'

'Yes, sorry to get you here so early, but I wanted to talk to you before the place got crowded and noisy.'

'Sure.'

As if on a given cue we both raised our glasses; synchronised drinking, I thought absurdly. Then I said, 'I saw Molly Richmond yesterday. She'd found the other part of Gwen's diary.'

'Oh yes, you told me about the one you read – wartime, on that farm somewhere.'

'Just outside Kidlington, near the airfield.'

'Was there anything in it – anything interesting?'

'Yes, it was very interesting. There was a photograph there too, and it made clear the one thing I hadn't had the wit to work out. It was, of course, an American airbase. The photograph was of the young girl, May Brown – you remember I told you about her? – and two American airmen. One was called Johnny – he was her boyfriend, the one who made her pregnant – the other was Johnny's friend Chuck.'

He made no comment so I went on.

'This part of the diary describes how Gwen Richmond saw this Chuck deliberately run down and kill May Brown one night when she had arranged to meet Johnny and insist that he should marry her. Why Johnny didn't do the deed himself I don't know. To judge from his photograph I don't think he had the stomach for it, though I'm sure he knew what his friend was up to.'

'You're right, that diary was interesting.'

'Gwen Richmond was a vindictive woman. She was also, in her own way, fond of poor little May. She decided to confront Chuck with what he had done – she didn't intend to go to the authorities, she preferred to have a personal hold over him – that's the sort of person she was. Unfortunately, from her point of view, she became ill and, by the time she had recovered, the American personnel had all been moved down to the south coast in the build-up to D-Day. But she was tenacious and I imagine she made enquiries and found out Chuck's name. Years later she ran into him, in the Bodleian, as it happens, and recognised him – surprisingly, after all these years. She confronted him with what she had seen that night and threatened to expose him. She had no proof, of course, apart from her diary – though that wouldn't stand up in a court of law and I don't suppose the other young man, Johnny, would have testified against his friend. But Chuck was now respected in his profession and established in a very select circle in the higher echelons of, shall we say, Boston society. The thought of this woman making noisy accusations, accusations that would be eagerly taken up by the media – have you noticed how fashionable anything about the Second World War is these days? – that would shatter his elegant lifestyle. Even if there is no proof, you know how avidly people listen to gossip. So that is why you set out to kill her.'

'I?'

'Yes. I believe Chuck might be an affectionate diminutive of Chester?'

'Can you imagine anyone calling *me* Chuck?'

'In certain circumstances, yes.'

'But, you're forgetting, I wasn't in Oxford the day she died. I went up to London by car with Jim – Dr Maxted – he's at St John's if you want to check. We left at eight-thirty in the morning – he likes to make a tediously early start – and we didn't get back until after midnight, because we went to the National – it was *The Seagull* – I think I told you about it.'

'And in between?'

'In between I worked in the British Library and Jim went to the Public Record Office.'

'Actually, in between, *you* went to Paddington and got a train back to Oxford.'

'You have proof of this?'

'Oh yes. Yesterday I happened to be clearing out my handbag – one accumulates such a lot of junk – and I came across those chocolate wrappers I rather officiously took away from you that afternoon in the Randolph. I am – I'm the first to admit it – an incurably nosy sort of person, so I smoothed out the wrappers to see what sort of chocolate you had been eating. In among them were two bus tickets. They're flimsy bits of paper, Oxford bus tickets, but they do have on them the date they were issued – and the date on those tickets was that of the day Gwen Richmond was murdered. I suppose you took a bus from the station into town and then back again after the murder to catch the train to London so that you could meet your friend – as I'm sure you arranged to – actually at the National before the performance.'

182

'What a pity you took the bus tickets away from me,' he said. 'Now they're not evidence – just your word against mine. In fact you haven't any *evidence* at all, have you?'

'No,' I said simply. 'I haven't. But you did kill her, didn't you? Because she saw you kill May Brown?'

'I suppose I could go on denying it, but, since you have no evidence – as she hadn't – and since it's just you and me – I suppose I must congratulate you on piecing things together so neatly. A successful piece of research, we might call it, though you won't be able to publish the results. And, really, she was a most unpleasant person – you know what she did to Fitz and Elaine. Now you must admit that the world is a better place without her.'

'I hold no brief for Gwen Richmond – she *was* unpleasant, though that doesn't give anyone the right to kill her. But it wasn't just her, was it? There was poor little May – and her unborn baby.'

He ran the tip of his finger around the rim of his glass and said, 'No, you're right – I shouldn't have done that. I suppose I was young and besotted, not that that's any excuse.'

'Besotted?'

'Johnny. It was what I believe they call a *coup de foudre* – I've never felt like that about anyone before or since – not even Fitz. There's something so very intense about first love, don't you agree?'

'Yes,' I said, 'first love can be like that.'

'He had no idea, of course; he thought we were *buddies*! You're right, he did call me Chuck. He used to find dates for me so that we could go out in foursomes! I guess people were pretty simple in those days.'

'I guess they were.'

'He was a strange sort of boy – rich and spoilt and very wild. His father was a general and really upset that Johnny had asthma and couldn't be a pilot and was just stuck as a second lieutenant in Supply on some cruddy little airbase in England. It sort of made Johnny defiant and he kept looking for ways to make his life seem more exciting. That's how he got into this black-market deal with the gasolene. It wasn't for the money, he was rolling, but for the kicks. Then this stupid little girl came along, whining that she was pregnant and saying that he had to marry her – there was no way he could do that, even if he'd wanted to. And then she tried to blackmail him over the gasolene deal. He couldn't bear the idea of facing his father if it all came out – he'd lose his allowance, sure, but it was much more than that – he was really terrified of the old man. He told me he'd agreed to meet the girl and I said I'd go instead and reason with her. I'd have done anything for him – I told you, I was obsessed – and, anyway, I was pretty crazy with jealousy over the whole affair. Of course he didn't know I did it deliberately. Even he might have smelled a rat if I'd told him that. I said it was an accident and we'd better just keep quiet. Then we got moved down to the south coast straight after – he'd forgotten about the whole thing by the end of the month.'

'Poor little May,' I said quietly. 'What happened to Johnny?'

'Killed in France – they machine-gunned the airfield. I guess,' he added wryly, 'the general would have been really proud to think his son had died in action.'

'It must have been quite a shock to discover someone had seen you that night.'

'Yes, the Richmond woman came up to me in the Bodleian one day and asked if I was Professor Howard. Then she said we had a mutual friend – May Brown. I'd practically forgotten the name, of course, and just stood there staring at her. Then she told me. She said something rather odd. She said she wasn't sure it was me until she saw me with my hat on.'

'Men change more completely as they get older,' I said, 'if they lose their hair. May Brown used to refer to you as James Mason – she was mad about films – so Gwen never really knew your name. It's funny, I noticed the other evening, when you put your hat on, that you reminded me of someone, I couldn't think who.'

'As you guessed, she'd found out my name all those years ago and now she threatened to make trouble. I couldn't have that – not just for me, but for Fitz – it would have brought the whole thing about Lance back to him.'

I was silent. Somehow I couldn't bring myself to tell Bill Howard what I had done to Fitz.

'I found out which room she was working in – I was lucky it was tucked right away like that. You were right about how I set my alibi with Jim Maxted and then came back by train – and bus – that was careless. I went along to her room. She was sitting at a desk and was surprised to see me. We talked for a while – I pretended to plead with her, to put her off her guard. She seemed quite relaxed and I remember she took her glasses off and put them away in their case. While her head was turned I took up that large metal-bound book and cracked it down on her head. I'm pretty tall and strong and she was – well – a little old lady, I guess. It didn't take that much to kill her. Then I loosened the screws in the bookshelves – I have always carried a penknife since I was a boy in summer camp, they surely do come in handy – and brought the ladder and the shelves down on top of her. As I say, I'm tall, so I was able to bring them down quite slowly so that there wasn't too much noise. Then I slipped away and – there you are. What should have been the perfect crime.'

'One thing I haven't worked out,' I said, feeling almost as if I were asking a question at the end of a seminar, 'is how you got in without George on the desk seeing you.'

'Human beings are pretty predictable,' he said, 'if they expect to see something they don't really notice it. If you look as though you've got a right to be somewhere people won't question you. I simply went round the back to the staff entrance about one o'clock when some of the staff were going out to lunch and some were coming back. I waited until a couple of people were coming out together, talking, and just went in – one of them even held the door open for me.'

'As easy as that!'

The pub was filling up now and getting noisier. Bill Howard looked at his watch.

'Well, it's been great talking to you,' he said. 'You're a good listener. You did a neat job, working it all out like that. Pity you haven't any evidence.'

Two figures came round from the next alcove, both were tall – one was very tall with red hair.

'Actually,' Michael said, 'we did hear every word. Confession before three witnesses. And just to make sure, we brought along William's new tape recorder – very high definition – state of the art, as they say. William says that will do as evidence.'

With sudden movement Bill Howard was on his feet. Involuntarily I cried out, 'Michael, be careful!' and then blushed with embarrassment as heads turned to look at me. Bill Howard laughed.

'It's all right,' he said, 'I'm not going to make a dash for it. No thrilling car chases down the Broad.'

Michael and William ushered him quietly but purposefully out of the pub. The car was parked at a meter a little way up St Giles and I unlocked the doors.

'If,' Bill Howard said, 'by any ridiculous chance the police should take this thing seriously, will you please tell Fitz what has happened.'

I shook my head.

'I'm sorry,' I said, 'but I don't think I could do that.'

Then we all got into the car and I drove us to the police station at St Aldates.

* * *

186

I leaned my hand against the warm stone of the archway that leads into the Schools quadrangle of the Bodleian.

SCHOLA ASTRONOMIAE ET RHETORICAE,
SCHOLA LOGICAE,
BIBLIOTHECA BODLEIANA

I would come back to Oxford, of course. But it would never be quite the same again.

920095

FIC   Holt, Hazel,
HOL   1928-

           The cruellest month.

$15.95

DATE			